On the Phone

A Novel

EVELYN GRILL
Translated by Renate Latimer

Translated from the German Ins Ohr, by Evelyn Grill (1942-),
Suhrkamp Verlag, Frankfurt am Main, 2002

Copyright © 2007 G. Meyer Books

Cover photo by Suzanne Mejean

Special thanks to the EUK in Straelen,
Christine Fritsch in Vienna, Karen Beckwith in Auburn,
and Cynthia Joan in Ann Arbor

Photo of Evelyn Grill courtesy of Suhrkamp Verlag

1.

In the Green Meadow

On our 20th wedding anniversary my husband had invited me to an elegant dinner. Although that was over two years ago, I still remember it as if it were yesterday. We sat in the casino-restaurant by candlelight and had already ordered our meal: I had asked for filets of milk-fed lamb, he a wiener schnitzel. What an affront to order a wiener schnitzel on our 20th wedding anniversary, by far the most vulgar dish in the Austrian cuisine. In my kitchen I have never fried one of these revoltingly common, and for every stomach-sensitive person, murderous pieces of meat, and so on our wedding anniversary he ordered this proletarian dish, with potato salad no less, offensive to my taste buds and my sense of style. Then my husband raised his glass and instead of saying: "To our future happiness" or "Thank you for all the years you've allowed me to spend with you" or, at the very least, "Cheers" or any appropriate saying a man with manners normally should have at his ready command on such occasions, he looked at me intently and said: "I'm taking this opportunity today to tell you that I'm planning to leave you. And so I'd like to drink with you to the years still lying ahead of us, and which we'll be spending apart." His words hadn't registered at all at first and I stared for a few seconds at his golden-yellow schnitzel and the little oily bubbles on the breadcrumb coating, at the slice of lemon and the little parsley twig, and I kept repeating his sentence to myself and felt that this could only be one of his—mind you, bad—jokes, and I gave a somewhat forced laugh. Then he smiled too and said he was glad I was receiving his suggestion so cheerfully and agreeably. I thought, well, that's great, if you intend to play such a tasteless game with me, then I'll simply play along too, although in the meantime I had lost my appetite for the delicious milk-fed lamb. "Ah," I said blithely, "something new at least. Do we want to get a divorce or simply have separate tables and beds?" Separate beds, though, had been a matter of course for years already, our sheets long since cut in two. After careful consideration he said he had decided to move out of our joint apartment for the time being; I was permitted to continue living there with our son, he would not yet seek a divorce at present, if I'd agree to an amicable and reasonable settlement. The most important thing for him was to be able to live alone and not have to see me on a daily basis. I looked at myself in the large mirror on the opposite wall, judged myself perfectly worthy of being seen, and asked myself why he no longer wanted to see me. Did I have leprosy? Did I exude a bad odor? Was I afflicted with deficiencies I had been unaware of until now? At any rate, it slowly dawned on me that he was serious. Close to tears I asked him what it was he so disliked about me. "Nothing," he said, "nothing, but I've had enough." I've had enough, he said, and I immediately remembered the Bach cantata one likes to play at funerals. On our 20th wedding anniversary our marriage was thus to be buried, to receive a first-class burial. So this was the funeral feast, with schnitzel and milk-fed lamb. You think something must have happened in our marriage? This decision of his must have had a pre-history? I should have noticed symptoms? But nothing had happened, nothing at all had happened, for years there had been no unpleasantness between us whatsoever. Except for my having passed, finally, after twenty semesters, my last law exam and I was just in the process of preparing for the bar exam while he had finally been promoted from Chief of Veterinary Medicine to Councilor. With the new title he had received a substantial pay raise and we wanted to send our son to boarding school in Bad Aussee, where he was to study for his university entrance exam. Supposedly I hadn't been able to pay sufficient attention to him, since every night I was sitting over my law books until four in the morning. I'd had to work through thousands of pages and store ten thousand paragraphs in my long-term memory. The law exams had been a snap compared to these challenges. The date for the bar exam was already scheduled for two months from now, and now of all times my husband had to decide on a separation, had to choose our anniversary to disclose his intention. Why then of all times still puzzles me today. You think it was pure cynicism, typical of men? No, he's not a cynic. In any case, I'd never been aware of such a trait in him until now. It was much worse, it was thoughtlessness, it was emotional brutality, and it was the perfect opportunity. Who knows, he probably thought, who knows when I'll have another chance like this where she's at my mercy—by candlelight, in public, where she can't make a scene, no tearful spectacle, she won't throw plates here in this elegant restaurant where we are known, the wine and exquisite food will soothe her, he probably thought, and by the time we're home she will have calmed down and tomorrow we can discuss the matter rationally. But don't forget that ever since my childhood I've suffered from a trauma, the trauma of abandonment. You say that psychotherapy or psychoanalysis might be helpful? Don't make me laugh. I tried that, years ago. Years ago I went to a psychoanalyst for that very reason, I sought out a shrink when my father the councilor-asshole abandoned us. He asked me immediately to lie down on his couch, and I was amazed because I assumed only the Sigmund Freud Museum still had a couch, but there it stood, it really still did exist, the psychoanalytic couch. However, it was a totally different model, without a carpet covering it, in blue and very simple, probably a Bauhaus design; the couch, you have to realize, is not a metaphor, but reality, and when I had reclined on the Knoll couch and taken off my shoes, a man's gentle voice told me to relax, to loosen up, close my eyes, breathe deeply in and out, ten times, and at the same time imagine that I was a tiny little girl standing in a meadow, all alone in a green meadow, and the meadow was carpeted with flowers and it stretched endlessly, and I was to tell him what associations I had, very quickly, that is, after I had counted to ten, and without thinking too much. And I tried to count to ten and to visualize at the same time a meadow and myself as a tiny little child in the meadow, and was proud that I succeeded with both right away, and so I stood in the green meadow and was all alone, as the soul-doctor had demanded, and I saw yellow dandelions, daisies, pink carnations, and bluebells at my little feet and with big eyes I looked up at the sky, which was so blue and the meadow so green and immeasurably big and deserted and I infinitely small; and then I began to cry. I think it's easier to cry when you're lying down than sitting or standing because it simply flows out of you while you are lying down, and the tears were indeed pouring down my cheeks and running into my ears and down my chin into my neckline and I briefly thought of my make-up, which my tears were now ruining, and I couldn't stop blubbering, and mucus was coming out of my nose and I couldn't breathe anymore and I sat up and gasped and doubled over and howled like a watchdog. When I finally had calmed down somewhat, I saw my therapist sitting there indifferent in his chair, nodding and observing me. This stranger had been staring at me the entire time, and had seen how I lost all my bearings in his green meadow. First he sent me to the green meadow and then he let me despair there. I came to my senses at last, jumped up, wiped the tears from my face, blew my nose, gathered my belongings together and shouted at him: "You perverse voyeur, you devious sadist!" or something like it, and with my shoes in my hand and slamming the door, naturally, I left his office. And for days afterwards I was ashamed of having let myself go like that in front of a complete stranger. It took me a long time to recapture, figuratively speaking, my tears, that is, to compose myself, and to cram all the painful images that had been lured to the surface and had been able to be lured forth so easily, deep back down. No, stop mentioning these soul-destroyers to me! None of these tormentors will ever see me again, I swear. By putting you on the couch they take you for a ride, with their sleazy-soft therapist voices they buzz into your ear, and right away you stand in the meadow and are delivered up to despair. Like Hansel and Gretel you are being led into the woods by these charlatans and then left alone. But in a fairy tale there is a happy ending; in psychoanalysis there is none. In short, with my schnitzel-eating partner who had bidden me farewell at my side, I felt as if I had been sent alone into the meadow. But I did not cry, I did not rage, I kept my cool this time—that is, not quite, because I began to laugh, rather loudly and rather long. I couldn't stop at all. The staff began to take notice. A waiter approached our table and I was still laughing. I was screaming with laughter and Walter hissed: "Stop it!" but I couldn't stop, and then Walter also began to laugh so that it wouldn't be so conspicuous, because a laughing man is something natural, but there's something disreputable about screeching women, and these elegant restaurants don't like to hear it. Women at most may giggle but to laugh so raucously and continuously, no, that was more than embarrassing. Therefore Walter saved the situation by joining me in my laughter. Yes, he even drowned out mine. It filled the space and room and my laughter finally faded into his. Then I could stop at last. I became silent, wiped the tears I had laughed from my face, and he gave me a stern look and I could feel his wounded pride because I regarded his intention to leave me as such a joke that I almost suffocated with laughter. Eventually, after I had renewed my make-up in the ladies' room, I asked him very soberly how he imagined a separation in practical terms; who would wash and iron his shirts and clean his shoes and cook his meals, and listen to him when he wanted to vent his anger from the office. And as I was formulating my question, I was already hoping again, no, I was actually convinced that the whole thing could only be one of his tactless jokes. But, lo and behold, he had already imagined a few things: he would rent his own, modest apartment. He longed for silence and seclusion. The laundry, he said, he'd drop off, of course, at my place. After all, he would still continue to pay for my apartment and my food. Could another woman have been in the picture? I'd have understood that. I'd have had something tangible to fight against. But unfortunately there was no evidence for that at all, at the time, I have to add in this case. He always came home punctually from the office and sat in the apartment. That is, of late he sat only in front of the computer and played solitaire, day after day, until bedtime. You know the game? Solitaire—every day. Before dinner and after,

Mr. Chief Veterinarian sat at his desk and played the game of patience on his monitor. I've been afraid for some time that this behavior of his would lead directly and inevitably to stupidity or insanity. Either he played solitaire or he was with his fraternity brothers somewhere. Women are strictly excluded from these male-bonding experiences so that the men can let it all hang out, or whatever. Right now, for example, he is sailing with them in the Mediterranean. My mother, who has hated him ever since he voiced his intention of leaving me (which he indeed did virtually overnight) was hoping he'd be washed overboard and drown in the Adriatic or be dismembered by sharks. One week before my bar exam, two months after his announcement of his decision to leave, he moved to the Mühlviertel, to a ridiculous hole of a village with the name of Engerwitzdorf. He had taken along his desk, his bed, his books, and of course his computer with the monitor, and left me sitting alone in the city apartment. He had dropped off his dirty shirts, naturally also his underwear and socks, because the washing machine as well as the iron remained with me. He stops by once a week to bring me his dirty laundry and exchange it for clean and ironed clothes. I had been stupid enough not only to agree to all this but also to cry my eyes out over him. The crying started at breakfast already which I suddenly had to eat all alone; I no longer had a conversation partner, no longer heard a human voice, and our son Mandi was at his boarding school in Bad Aussee meanwhile from where he was writing me desperate letters. You ask whether I had loved Walter so much? That's irrelevant now. I married him. He is still my husband. One doesn't question love or non-love. It's simply a private-legal contract that we drew up together. *Pacta sunt servanda*: An implicit duty to stand by each other *for better or for worse*. Of course I no longer loved him, he had long since gotten on my nerves, and I was stupid on the whole to miss him at all because I can't even tell you exactly what it was I missed about him. I didn't miss him personally; he had mainly been a stand-in for my fear of being alone and abandoned, which had solidified into a complex ever since my visit to the analyst and which had been implanted in me since childhood; well, you know the story of my father, the veritable councilor, he too…and the green meadow, you understand! Sex, no, he hadn't slept with me for years, I told you already—for years no sex at all. What, you think he might have become impotent? Yes, you are right, once he did have a bilateral inflammation of both testicles. First he had mumps, then inflammation of the testicles. His balls were as big as a bull's at the time. So swollen, and painful. You think there could have been an after-effect—erectile dysfunction as a late development? Men would rather take flight and retire to remote retreats as semi-recluses and play solitaire or, to ward off oppression, play Minesweeper on their PCs to avoid admitting a weakness? You think it might be a matter of male sense of shame? I couldn't have cared less had he been impotent. I was busy enough with my studies. But now I'm worried I may not be getting any more money. He's beginning to calculate every penny he's depositing into my account so that I now have little freedom of movement. He said he now had two households to support and my housekeeping money would therefore have to be less generous than before. And if you're without a husband your social status plunges immediately; then you're no longer Frau Councilor here and Frau Councilor there. The mailbox usually stays empty and invitations to private parties are rare, too, as soon as the news leaks out that you are available, so to speak, again and therefore a threat to the hostess-wives. You think that's provincial? Well, believe me, that's how it still is in this small town. Of course I'm still in touch with him, amicably, by telephone, and dealing with his dirty laundry, as he demanded. Sometimes he even takes me out to dinner to some kind of a pub in the Mühlviertel where you get smoked pork with sauerkraut or noodles with cabbage, or wiener schnitzel of poor quality and wine that gives you a headache the next day. He says he has discovered the simple life. Recently he called me again because he wanted to know whether Mandi had finally passed his high school exams. Of course he passed; I had brought him home again so that I wouldn't be so alone. The child was so happy. I'm still reproaching myself for even having sent him away to boarding school because I thought I'd have too little time for him. But one always finds time for what's important. In the fall, Mandi has to do his military duty and afterwards he wants to study. And then he'll be a full-fledged member of the Danubia Fraternity and will get drunk regularly with his fraternity brothers and his father and thus establish his professional career. Gay? What makes you think that? Latently gay? Who are you talking about? The father? Oh no. Why would he turn gay all of a sudden? A councilor can't take such chances. Yes, depressed. Definitely depressed. Threatened by inner chaos. Therefore the non-stop solitaire and never Minesweeper, at least not while we were still together. He arranged his world on the monitor. Maybe I shouldn't have undertaken my third course of studies. The more progress I made in my studies, the more our marital ways parted. I wasn't even aware of our estrangement. In fact, I do remember now, he began to play solitaire after I had passed my first diploma exam and was furiously aiming for the final law exams. At the beginning of my studies he had always made light of my endeavors and let me have my way. He, the tenured veterinarian, had observed my housewifely studies–that's how he referred to it—good-naturedly but from a distance, as long as everything functioned well at home. And things did function. When I think of all I accomplished—I sewed my own dresses, even my suits, and still make them today. Night after night I studied and sewed and cooked and mended and washed and ironed, night after night. And barely slept a wink. What was I supposed to do alone in bed, the husband on his PC playing solitaire? Maybe I shouldn't have undertaken a course of studies so late? He might have handled social studies or German studies, but not law. I should not have penetrated his male domain. Perhaps my incursion into his male world threatened him in his sovereignty; just imagine, a wife, a housewife and mother, hierarchically on society's lowest rung, undertakes to climb the ladder, to approach the head of the household at eye level–to a certain degree I can even understand his sentiments–or wouldn't you be annoyed if your cleaning woman, whom you could order around and even torment for years, suddenly wanted to be addressed as "Frau Doktor" because she stealthily completed her university studies? It's easy to lose one's orientation then, particularly if you are a man. I called his natural superiority into question, robbed him of his identity. I'm not afraid to move on and up. With my master's degree I castrated him, metaphorically speaking. Most likely he has been searching for a new identity ever since I passed my final law exams. What am I supposed to do? I fear I've paid all too high a price for my university degree. You think I have gained a lot, approval, satisfaction, from my studies? You think it was fun for me? No, it wasn't fun at all, not for a single moment did I have fun. But I couldn't break it off, my mother had already informed our entire circle of acquaintances and friends that her daughter was studying law, and now I was constantly being asked about the progress of my studies by both well-meaning and ill-disposed people. Some smiled condescendingly at my efforts. My mother-in-law likewise felt that a wife and mother should know her place and not deprive her husband of his domestic comforts with her intellectual ambition since he was the one bringing home the money which enabled her to lead a comfortable housewifely existence. These and similar comments had spurred my ambition immensely; soon I studied only out of resistance to my surroundings because, in fact, the entire legal rubbish didn't interest me in the least; it still doesn't interest me today, and yet I suddenly faced the bar exam and there was no turning back. I was so afraid of failing and embarrassing myself should I fail. I'll definitely fail, I kept on thinking; I had no idea how I was to master the entire material, during the day in the law office of Zappatotti who was exploiting me as his legal assistant, and at night, alone, with my lecture notes. I don't even know why I'm telling you all this, because it's over now. I did in fact pass the bar exam; I have my lawyer's certification in my pocket, but instead of rejoicing after the exam I descended the wide staircase of the courthouse and burst into tears. What now, I thought, what now, I have to become a lawyer now and open an office and woo clients and defend them and win trials, and I can't even afford a secretary, nor can I afford an office, and I felt I was ready now for the psychiatric ward or for suicide. And that's how things stand at present. Tell me I'm stupid, or tell me what I should do, and Walter also congratulated me and invited me to the Auhof Restaurant for pork roast with dumplings, and I wanted him so much to come home with me, just as he used to, but he returned to the Mühlviertel and I to the city. And Mandi is in the army, with the pioneers, and Walter said I had now reached my goal, and my mother said that she'd be my secretary in my office, which I can't even afford. And as I was sitting alone at my kitchen table I felt that Walter's words that I had now reached my goal were nonsense; I haven't reached my goal at all, I don't even want to reach my goal, but rather I was just at the beginning, but the beginning of what I didn't know.

2.

On the Nile

Actually I couldn't really spare the time, but I had promised Mandi a trip after he finished his military service and before he began his studies. He wanted to take a cruise. His father reproached me with a reproving look, saying that our son was still an obvious loner; this man thinks I'm responsible for everything just because Mandi happens to live with me. But I told Walter that a son's initiation was a father's duty even among the savages, and he should set a good example for him by showing him the art of seducing women. That was malicious of me because I knew that the councilor had become, or maybe always had been, much too wooden to seduce. He immediately disputed his responsibility, saying it sufficed that he took Mandi along on sailing tournaments he organized with his fraternity brothers, real men, that those were sufficient examples and lessons for life, he couldn't do more than that, he had, after all, a career, and Mandi also had a mother. And it was with me, I suddenly realized, that my son also wanted to be on the water. Maybe in the watery element he detected or wanted to detect a common bond between his separated parents. Not long ago, as I was standing in the kitchen by the stove stirring a sauce; Mandi suddenly stood behind me and kissed me on the neck, on the side, on the left. I've always had the habit of holding my head slightly at an angle. And so I evidently showed him my unprotected flank. I have a long neck, a swan's neck as one used to call it. It irritated me to suddenly feel his mouth, his soft lips on this sensitive spot. I was even startled a little because I hadn't even noticed him standing behind me. It's not, after all, an everyday occurrence that a grown son kisses his mother on the neck. Is it? And I immediately searched my memory when a man had last kissed me on the neck and I couldn't come up with anything. In any case, I told my son he was supposed to treat girls that way, not his mother. And so I realized now I had to undertake the promised trip with him, although this particular moment was extremely unfavorable in another regard since I had finally found an office. A lawyer in Kremsmünster was retiring and wanted to entrust me with his office under favorable conditions. It is located right next to the world-famous high baroque monastery, on the second floor, the ideal floor, and on the first floor is a delicatessen, which is a good thing because people stop and look and see not only the Spanish wine, Italian Prosecco, and French blue cheeses but also my sign. My mother said I couldn't possibly take a trip now. I had to set up my office, otherwise when I returned from the Nile someone else would have ruined my business. She said she likes the office. She can see herself sitting in there, picking up the telephone receiver and bringing me clients or keeping them away from me, as the case may be. I was quite taken aback by her vigor because it was my decision, after all, and I was annoyed that with her hectic activities she wanted to spoil a trip that I myself was actually reluctant to take, particularly at this time. But I had promised Mandi and there happened to be a special offer on the luxury liner *Egypt*. I had booked everything already, and now there was no backing out and my mother immediately offered to take charge of everything. She knew, after all, what I wanted, and when we returned everything would be settled. Ever since my mother's last lover went astray and she gave up looking for a successor, the purpose of her whole life has become organizing my office and being her daughter's secretary. I didn't much object to that, because I couldn't have afforded a secretary in the beginning. Yet at the same time I had an uneasy feeling about granting her so much influence so early in my freelance legal career, and therefore I would have liked to call off the trip altogether–promises or no promises– and with a cancellation I would have irritated above all my husband the councilor because it was he above all who urged me to travel with Mandi now. I noticed, you see, that it was my activities regarding the establishment of my office that irritated him. Whenever he brought me his dirty shirts to be laundered he always said that I had now reached my goal, as if I could now take it easy, but I said, no, this was just the beginning. "If only you don't fall flat on your face with your own office," he said. "I'm not going to vouch for you at a bank because I don't want to encourage you in your recklessness," said he, a civil servant, who naturally disdains every kind of insecurity that free enterprise brings with itself. He also infected me somewhat with his security-obsessed councilor's mentality. Or maybe my grandparents and parents already infected me from birth. Everything had proceeded without risk. The career ladders were set up, and one simply had to climb them step-by-step. For my ancestors, there was no turning back and no descent. There existed only progress, and the goal was the councilor, the highest achievement, likewise on the salary scale. But what I was planning had no safety net but was a plunge into cold water in my advanced years, and my husband would observe and comment from his Mühlviertel-hellhole or from his Office for Veterinary Affairs on my toiling in the free market economy, which is never a social one. But now I was simply to travel with Mandi to the Nile and fulfill my maternal duties. "He's a veritable manly little wallflower, your son," he said. "He doesn't even loosen up during our drinking sessions." So I thought how is the man supposed to coax the son into the open if he himself is unable to coax anything out of himself—this monitor gawker, this solitaire gazer. And for the first time I was happy that I was rid of him and thought to myself: *Those dirty shirts of his won't be washed much longer*. We chose our cabins on the upper deck, which wasn't exactly cheap, but I wanted to be generous and besides, I assumed our fellow-travelers, with whom we had to spend the next ten days after all, would be correspondingly cultivated. Don't expect me to tell you about the pyramids, the Nile scenery, the ruins of Memphis, the Arabic cemetery of Minich, the graves of the sheiks, the temple of Hathor, the temple layout of Karnak, and the many other temple mounds. On the third day I was already weary of seeing. I couldn't take in anything more, I was so stunned by so much past and history. Soon I felt so insignificant and ridiculous in the face of the thousand-years-old culture that I was greatly tempted not to plan anything anymore for the banal present. Therefore I tried to immunize myself against the cultural monuments, the landscape, the sunrises and sunsets. And I began to search on our deck for suitable partners for my son. When he begins his studies in Innsbruck in the fall, forestry of all things, he should bring some experience with him, otherwise he won't have the appropriate access to his studies. We were assigned a table with couples only, not a single young girl in sight. Finally I discovered a whole group of fidgety teenies at one of the more distant tables. I was looking for one particular one whom I could invite to our table after the rigid seating arrangement relaxed. Mandi enjoyed the food and seemed very content. Food, on the whole, means quite a lot to him, perhaps too much. On the third evening, we docked near Luxor, a starry sky as if in a fairy tale. I spotted a girl sitting alone at a table. She was quite pretty. I asked her to join us at our table. Her name was Anita and she came from East Tyrol, from the vicinity of Lienz, and we came from the vicinity of Linz; there was a little laughter, Linz and Lienz, it was almost a stroke of fate. The boat's band had already begun to play; I could therefore leave the two alone, but not without first ordering a bottle of champagne for them. Maybe my intention to depart was a bit too abrupt because the girl gave me a surprised look and I had to excuse myself, I was tired and also had a migraine. Mandi (I could tell from his tense posture) would have liked nothing better than to accompany me. I wished them a fun evening, made the point once more that I didn't feel good, but that they shouldn't therefore let their mood be spoiled, and I withdrew. In my cabin, as I was relaxing in my bath, I realized the evening was still quite young. And so I would have to wait for a long time for Mandi to give me an account on the following morning. But perhaps he wouldn't tell me anything. A gentleman is silent and savors. I tried to read in our guidebook but I couldn't concentrate because I remembered my office in Kremsmünster, I was skeptical that my mother would be able to manage things and regretted that I hadn't postponed the trip. Now that it was a matter of my very existence, I had sought out the water, worried about my son's love life instead of setting up my legal practice. In order to force myself to think of other things I got dressed again, crept into the upper deck and peered into the dance hall. I hid behind a leafy tropical plant. The boat's band played a wild samba, and on the dance floor I immediately discovered Anita with a young dandy. I was momentarily panic-stricken; what had happened to my son? He was still sitting at our table and staring into his champagne glass. The expression on his face—as a mother, after all, I can read his face like no one else—was enough to melt a heart of stone. After this dance there came a cha-cha-cha, and then the Valentino-imitator guided Anita to the bar. She hadn't even glanced at Mandi who was still staring at his half-full bottle of champagne. I could have strangled this Anita and her admirer. Who was she anyway? Most likely she came from extremely modest circumstances—from Lienz, where most likely only the most modest circumstances existed—and she, in her getup, a hairdresser at best. Yes, assuredly, one of these uneducated curlers of locks. The next day at breakfast I acted depressed: "I believe this Anita wasn't the right one for you after all. How did you manage to get rid of her?" Mandi, who at first had stared bleakly at his breakfast egg, was revived. He hurled himself onto the golden bridge that I had erected for him. He had never encountered anything so mega-dumb as Anita. And with such a thing I had expected him to spend an entire evening. That annoyed him. He had asked her to dance one time because he couldn't stand her jabbering any longer. "You even danced with her!" I exclaimed with surprise. He gestured disapprovingly: she had zero sense of rhythm. "I'm sorry," I said. "Did you ask her what she did?" "Hairdresser," Mandi said disgustedly. I seized my son's hand, caressed it, and he beamed at me. And although I had seen him sitting there desperately unhappy and abandoned I believed for a moment every word he said. Imagine that! I accepted all his lies and deceptions and was grateful for them. Later on I learned that this Anita is the daughter of an architect and is studying in Vienna at the University of Applied Arts.

But naturally I also kept that from Mandi. The rest of the trip we were soul mates again. From time to time the beauty crossed our path but we punished her by ignoring her. Not until we were heading home did I have misgivings about the correctness of my behavior. I resolved to have a serious, brutally honest discussion with the veterinarian about our son's inhibitions. But just imagine, he didn't even let me get a word in: I shouldn't act so sanctimonious because, according to Mandi, who had told him in strict confidence, I myself, with my boundless jealousy, had driven away all the pretty young girls who intended to approach him or whom he intended to approach, with my pointed comments, afterwards badmouthing them to him. My son didn't have a single hour to himself. And what did I reply after I found words again? Nothing. I can't very well make my son out as a liar to his father, can I? Or what was I supposed to have done?

3.

My Mother and I

I found her. She was sitting in the chair she had recently acquired, a Marcel Breuer club chair in black leather, expensive and comfortable; she was proud of it, and she was still holding the telephone receiver in her hand. A peeping sound emerged from it, but otherwise everything was silent, and my mother was resting her head on the desktop so at first I thought she had fallen asleep, and I was annoyed because she had been so absentminded of late, couldn't remember anything, least of all the names of my clients who unfortunately weren't all that numerous yet. She was also confusing all my appointments and I thought to myself as I saw her lying there, now she's even falling asleep on the job in broad daylight, I really can't use her anymore, yet I still need her, I can't afford a secretary yet and someone has to sit in the waiting room and greet the clients and answer the telephone. When you are starting out you have to be accommodating to people, be obliging, a telephone answering machine won't do; clients immediately want to be addressed in person, want human contact and not a machine, and so she lay there and seemed to be asleep, whereas in fact she was almost gone. I shouted at her. "Mother," I screamed, "that does it!" Yes, I'm ashamed. I shouted at a dying woman, my mother, because I was annoyed. That is, I was half annoyed and half afraid, actually I was very afraid, I was enormously frightened, and I placed my annoyance into my voice and thus suppressed my fear, because naturally I somehow sensed at once that something terrible, something unimaginably dreadful had happened and that my mother had not fallen asleep but rather was already half-dead. I grabbed her by the shoulders and shook her and placed her on the Berber rug in my office, put her on her side because I remembered my first-aid course, and ran to the telephone and called the ambulance; that is, mistakenly I dialed the emergency police number and they thought a murder had taken place in my office because I was talking so confusedly, but then everything was cleared up and I dialed the correct number. Until the arrival of the ambulance I listened to my mother's breathing, which was still faint, called out her name, caressed her, placed my ear on her chest and could still hear the beating of her heart and I kept pleading: "Dear God, you mustn't take my mother away. Dear God, I beg of you, don't let her die!" and all sorts of other things one stammers under the circumstances, one loses utter control, and when the rescue team showed up I was so worked up that the physician immediately gave me a sedative because in my state of confusion I might have hampered their emergency treatments. After this sedative I soon became quite calm, yes, apathetic, and then I fell asleep in the office on the Biedermeier chaise longue, which my mother had forced on me. When I woke up I was disoriented at first and only gradually did I recall everything. I panicked, called the Protestant Hospital where they had taken my mother. It took a long time, let me tell you, to be connected with the right place, and finally someone, a female voice, explained to me that my mother was in surgery, that is, an operation was being prepared, some emergency surgery, a minor intervention procedure. I was oddly relieved and drove off to the hospital to wait for my mother to awake from the anesthesia. This surgery gave me hope and yet I hadn't even inquired as to what and where the operation was, I was so groggy from the sedative that this stupid doctor had given me. During the hours I spent sitting on a hard bench in the hallway of the hospital and waiting for my mother, it seemed to me as if I were watching the entire misery of mankind passing before me. Most of all I would have liked to run away, outside into the park, into nature, to the flowers and the hopping and skipping children with their smooth chubby faces and healthy joints, and far away from the hobbling shapes in flapping hospital gowns, and it wasn't until now that I remembered my son who was studying in Innsbruck the past few months, and I reached for my cell phone and rushed outside to the parking lot to call him. But he wasn't available and I sent him my cry for help as a text message. Then I rushed back in order not to miss my mother's return. She was brought back finally; they pushed her toward me along the long hallway. I didn't even recognize her; the doctor said it was my mother but I saw a stranger, an old woman who didn't concern me, but the doctor said they had to remove a small tumor from my mother's brain, a tumor, he said. And I kept thinking: *What have they done with my mother? This can't be my mother*, and I wanted to shout the words into his face, "You have murdered my mother," but I said nothing and in a daze walked alongside the cot with the railing, which the nurses continued to push down the hall, and I kept searching for something familiar in this alien face with its bald, shorn head, the sunken lips, the pointed nose. It was this bald skull with its bluish skin that horrified me so much, and on the place where they evidently had drilled a hole, a white bandage was stuck, and the mouth of this moribund form, which was supposed to be my mother, was askew on its face, which looked angry and disdainful. My mother never had such an expression in her face. The eyelids were open only a little crack, through which I saw the whites of her eyeballs. And still the nurses and the doctor were hurrying with her bed through the hall, and I thought I would be forever condemned to run alongside this bed, but finally they pushed the patient into a tiny room which didn't even have a window, and when I looked around I realized it had to be a storage room because there were shelves stacked with bedpans, diapers, bandages and rubber gloves. I wanted to protest that my mother was stored away in a windowless closet; fluorescent lights glared from the ceiling, pitilessly, illuminating everything, including my mother's yellow face, but the doctor pushed a chair toward the bed and said I could stay until the patient awoke. If anything unexpected should arise I should press a certain button; whereupon he and the nurses vanished through the door. And so I sat by the bed of my mother who didn't move, and tried to recognize her again and prayed and began to caress her through the railing of her cot, this person so dreadfully alien with the repulsive facial expression, and I still felt the warmth of her body and I took her still familiar hands. I recognized her bony, strong hands and her well-groomed, pink, polished nails, she always insisted on manicured nails, and I massaged her feet and joyfully discovered her chilblains and the ingrown toenail on her left big toe and the corn on her right little one, and then I was happy because now her face no longer seemed like a stranger's; I recognized the eyebrows which she always had meticulously plucked, and her chin with the dimple, and I put my hands under the cover and caressed her breasts and stomach and pushed my hands under the small of her back, and everything was still warm and full of hope, and I talked to her incessantly and I even thought I saw a facial muscle twitching a little and the slanting mouth had straightened up a bit, but suddenly a little stream of saliva ran out of the corner of her mouth. It was pink and then turned red and I pressed the button like crazy and ran outside into the hall and called for the doctor. I should have remained sitting there by her side because when the doctor and I approached her bed my mother had opened her eyes wide and stared at the ceiling and her lower jaw had dropped down as if she had uttered one last cry. Perhaps she would have cast one last glance at me or spoken a word, or found a syllable at least, if I had stayed with her in the moment of her death; for it was obvious she was dead and yet I still couldn't grasp it because she was still warm and this very morning she had suggested we visit a new chic furniture store, I can't think of its name right now, it displays only designer pieces; she was insistent on buying me a special desk, the furnishing of my office was virtually the only thing on her mind the last few months, and that's why she had really gotten on my nerves; I had barely accustomed myself to a piece of furniture when she came with a new suggestion. She visited galleries to purchase pictures that pleased her and to decorate the walls of my office with; most recently she dragged in a huge oil painting which, until now, had adorned the wall above the sideboard in her living room: a portrait of my grandmother, a citizen of Steyr, eminent and esteemed because of her husband, my grandfather, a pathologist and the first councilor in our family. A huge reddish fox fur was draped around her shoulders and around her throat a pearl choker that is now in my possession and which I'm in the habit of wearing during important hearings to impress the judges and district attorneys. This, my stately ancestor, was supposed to be resplendent behind my desk, looking on the one hand over my shoulders and on the other hand into my clients' faces, thus emphasizing the competence of his legally erudite granddaughter. Since I was so busy with other things at the time I objected only half-heartedly to the painting, indulged my mother, although this pretentious oil painting with the severe-looking progenitor annoyed me and I was thinking that as soon as I had established myself somewhat I would take it down again. But now that my mother is dead, dead from one hour to the next, I'll leave it where it is, I can't part anymore with this abomination in its bombastic baroque gold frame. When I remember how unkind, yes, insufferable I was to Mother of late, I'll just pay my final tribute to her with this hideous monstrosity. That'll ease my bad conscience a little. And so many things in general which she had arranged and set up in my office I can't undo, now that she is gone and can't contradict me. Do you understand? I, in any case, understand nothing anymore, not myself and not death. But you're right, who does understand death? But to understand a mother's death is most difficult and most impossible. I saw her lying there; in the morning she was still full of plans and in the evening she was dead, but still warm. She still had the familiar smell, the mother-smell, and I wanted to crawl into her bed, but she lay in a bed with a railing and I asked the doctor to let me lie down beside my mother to keep her warm but the physician said she was already dead and the dead would be put promptly in a coffin and taken to the morgue and kept cold and not warm. That was the custom here. Finally he granted me three hours because the storage room was not used by anyone anyway but the nursing staff and her body would not be in anyone's way. And so I gathered together all my remaining strength and flung into his face the words that he was a heartless physician and I was an attorney and he would be hearing from me. I lowered the railing and crawled into my mother's bed and caressed her and couldn't stop calling: "Mama, Mama, Mama." And that's how my son found me. My text message had already reached him, he was on his way home, which was quite fortunate since he had planned to come home today anyway, and he approached the bed, and I noticed he was completely bewildered by my childish behavior. But I couldn't stop. Finally he cried out in desperation: "Some restraint, Mama, I beg of you, please, restraint!" Those were the words I used to resort to when he was about to lose control or had already lost it. And so I crawled out of my mother's bed. She had grown cold and rigid in the meantime and had begun to exude a strange smell, a smell of death; I had not been able to prevent or impede this process with my bodily warmth, and I threw myself into my son's arms who stroked my back reassuringly and found loving words so that I wept even more profusely, but it was no longer as painful. Had I not had Mandi, I don't even know how I would have gotten over all that. Finally I had to allow them to take my mother away to the cold storage chamber and we had to make arrangements for the funeral. I had to close the office for one day, the day of the funeral, on account of death in the family. All other days I kept the business running. Only in the evenings after I came home did I start to cry, and only after I had shed the quantum of tears I had to suppress during the day and my swollen eyes grew shut so that I was virtually blind, was I able to eat something and talk to my son who did not leave my side during these difficult hours. I discussed everything with him, even who was to receive the obituary announcements. We arranged a lovely, first class funeral, with music and everything that goes with it, and a funeral banquet at the Tabor Restaurant. But only a handful of relatives turned up, there simply weren't many left, and a few of my mother's girlfriends who told me how proud she had always been of me and had loved me above all else. Once again a flood of tears, and I recalled how I had lately mistreated my poor mother. One time when she had forgotten once again to call someone important or to cancel an appointment I had insulted her by calling her feebleminded. In fact, of late, all she did have on her mind was the furnishing of my office, rearranging the furniture, which she had bequeathed to me and which was now immovable. I had also survived the day of her funeral, which, strictly speaking, was more difficult to survive than the day of her death, and now I had to seek refuge in my sorrow alone since Mandi was returning to Innsbruck. First of all I took a bath and used my mother's bubble bath, which I could never bear to smell but whose scent now delighted me and brought tears back to my eyes. Suddenly I saw my naked body in the mirror with entirely different eyes. Suddenly I felt so old, everything was so flabby: my arms, my thighs, and I had lost weight, I hadn't eaten anything the last few days, I only smoked, and in this emaciated body I could very well imagine the skeleton I would one day, maybe quite soon, turn into, for I'll be next in line. As long as you have a mother you don't think of the possibility of death, because first it's the mother's turn, that's the silent agreement with fate, which I as a daughter had made, and now I had lost this protection; now I was standing in the front row, I could keel over at any time, that's how I was feeling especially with this gaunt body of mine with its shriveled skin, and I felt the end of everything, my life and my expectations, and the hopelessness of it all. I lay down in the warm water and thought of Seneca and of opening my veins. That is supposed to be a nice death. But most likely also a big mess when they'd find me, lying in my blood, disgusting. After the bath I quickly dried myself off and avoided looking in the mirror. I swallowed a tranquilizer and dropped into sleep. But on the following morning, I woke up and was in despair once again because I didn't know how to go on without my mother, and now I still had to look for a new secretary. Who would listen to me from now on? I can call you again, can't I?

4.

The Shirt

For years my mother had urged me to find a lover; it was unnatural for a woman my age to be brooding over documents at home night after night and then to lie alone in bed. My mother had always pressured me to acquire an admirer, at least a "kiss-your-hand-admirer" who would enhance my reputation in society; it was high time to forget about this councilor to whom I had been married *de jure* for twenty-five years and who during the last five years did not, *de facto* touch me before he took off, which understandably humiliated me, although as far as I remember I always used to dread his announcement during breakfast of his desire for copulation that evening. I was sick the entire day whenever I thought of the impending event because instead of an act of love it always turned into a bureaucratic act with which he deposited duly and dutifully his seed in me. And now it was legal acts that filled my days and nights. I went to bed with them and rose with them. Once a well-to-do financial lawyer from Carinthia whom I liked quite a bit wanted to have a candlelight dinner with me at a local pub. I decided to accept the invitation, dressed up, looked at myself from every angle in the tall mirror in the hallway, was pleased, walked to the door, held the doorknob in my hand, let go and returned to my legal documents. The more insistently my mother demanded a man from me, the more I resisted. I had my office and my mother as my secretary. That sufficed. I worked like a maniac for my clients, and my mother was on the lookout for a lover for her daughter. I couldn't understand that. Through my father (the first councilor-asshole in the family, the veterinarian mutated years later into the second one) she had, after all, experienced enough disappointments and humiliations, until he finally had left her. And her subsequent lovers likewise, with whom she demonstrated dubious taste, caused her only trouble which I as her daughter was forced to share. And she, she of all people, demanded a lover of me. She gave up finally: "OK, if you don't want a man, why don't you keep a dog at least?" And so I got myself a dog—a greyhound, a black Afghan. He was exceptionally decorative and not particularly cheap, matched my hair color; matched my personality, as a passer-by recently told me. Imagine this: I was strolling in Steyr in the market square and the dog unfortunately had an excessive urge to be in motion and lacked all training since I was incapable of training a dog. One has to be an authoritarian type who likes to shout: "Sit! Stop! No!" Well, the dog jerked me along on his leash and I, half-running, breathless, with flying hair, following him, still wearing my beige-colored Armani suit (I had long since stopped sewing my own clothes). This guy approached me, grinning, and said: "The dog becomes you." The dog becomes me! Mandi, too, my son, wanted me to get a dog. "You won't be so defenseless, Mama," he said, "and you'll have someone to protect you when you walk around alone at night, in parking lots or parking structures." But I'm never out alone at night. And yet I ended up with this beast, it followed me about everywhere, even when I went to the bathroom it sat in front of the door and whimpered, it did all sorts of things but it did not protect me. The mutt, whose straggly fur had to be brushed for hours every day, liked the face of every stranger, wagged its tail cajolingly, and wanted to be petted incessantly. All of which led me into quite a few embarrassing situations because some men, whom the animal approached with a wagging tail and masochistic submissiveness, sized me up suspiciously; I saw distrust in their eyes and read their thoughts that I had trained the dog to approach them. But the description stated that our Afghan greyhound was an aristocratic animal and kept an aloof distance from strangers. Something must have gone awry in the breeding of mine. Besides, my black Afghan was not a male but a bitch. She scented her master in every male; her groveling behavior disgusted me. She followed me into the bedroom, jumped into my bed. Later on at night I locked her into the broom closet so that I wouldn't have to hear her whimpering. And her smell! Dogs always do smell abominably. But it didn't begin to bother me until after I had the shirt. Before the shirt I wasn't aware of it. The shirt? Let me tell you about it, I need your advice. All right then, my mother had died two months earlier. I couldn't get over her loss at all. Almost every day after work I drove out to the cemetery and lit a new candle. I felt so abandoned. I had the feeling everything was slipping out of my hands. Barely eight weeks after my mother was in her grave I met this man, a mechanical engineer, at a hearing before the District Court in Engelhartszell. He was an expert witness in my case. After the hearing we went to a country inn to have a bite. Nothing happened at this point. Two days later he called and asked me if he could send me an e-mail. It began quite harmlessly. The e-mails quickly turned intimate, more and more imaginative and affectionate, in short, more and more passionate. I could barely wait to open my Inbox and check the messages. When we saw each other again I was so wrought up that I fell into his arms like an overripe fruit. So now I have a lover, a Latin lover, that's what I secretly call him because he's so dark. No, not black. He has dark curly hair, a southern type, Mediterranean somehow, but still, a genuine Austrian, a handsome man. His name is Wolfram. I call him Wolf, my wild animal. He only had to invite me to dinner once after my mother was barely dead and already I accepted all his invitations to dinner, already I had fallen under his spell. And ever since there has been turmoil and chaos, I live, I die, I burn and I freeze. My mother would be pleased? You think it's wonderful? You have no idea how stressful it is. I can't be without the man. I've never experienced anything like it, least of all with the veterinarian. Let me tell you, I bought alluring lingerie for the first time in my life and I spent a fortune. You have to help me, I've got to get out of this, tell me I'm sick, that I'm crazy. I'm fifty-two, imagine that. I'm at Victoria's Secret. I'm rummaging among the lingerie, red lace, black, and flesh-colored. The saleswoman, an innocent young thing, asked me: For you? I almost blushed and would have slunk off shamefacedly, but then this young and dumb and pretty and wrinkle-free face annoyed me so much that I said no, not for me, for my mother. The smile froze on her face. Embarrassed now she eagerly heaped panties, bras and garters onto the sales table. All the items available! And Victoria's

Secret isn't even remotely as racy as Beate Uhse. I also ended up buying a see-through negligee in Bordeaux-red. That goes well with my black hair. But I wouldn't have needed it because he immediately tore off all my clothes, ripped them off, my ripping wolf, he didn't even bother to look at my expensive lingerie. You think that's normal, at my age? My Wolfram. My Wolf—my wild animal. And he's eleven years younger than me. 41! In the prime of life! Sometimes I think when I'm 62, he'll be 51. I'll be an old hag and he'll still be in the best years of his life. There's no future there. You have to talk me out of him. I'm 72. He's 61. You can count, can't you? You think it makes no difference? He's so good-looking he could get any young woman he wanted. He could get ten on each finger. You can't imagine how affectionate he is, and so gentle. And his skin…I love his skin, and his smell! And he always asks me if it's all right, if I'm fine—too warm, too cold? Would I like a shawl around my shoulders? And every day when I come to the office I check to see if he sent me an e-mail. It has become a ritual. He's so imaginative, so sensitive. He admitted bashfully that he's a passionate reader of lyric poetry. He needed it as a compensation for his prosaic profession, to refuel his soul. Isn't that unusual for a mechanical engineer and car dealer? Everything is unusual about him. This is the third e-mail he sent me, and one I'll never forget:

> *If today I do not touch your body*
> *Then my soul's thread will tear*
> *Like a string too tautly stretched.*
> *May coolness soothe my feverish brow*
> *As I lean unsteadily outside.*

His soul's thread will tear! You have to imagine that figuratively. It has stirred me up so much. Do you know that feeling? I haven't discovered yet who the poet is. He won't tell me, I have to find out myself. Tell me I'm crazy. I immediately drove out to St. Pölten to see him. After our first night of love he made me a present of his shirt. Another e-mail was brief and to the point: *How I called you, you primeval mountain of desire!* How am I supposed to resist! He's so different from all other men. He goes shopping with me and looks on patiently when I'm indecisive in my selections. He stops before every shop window as long as I want to. We spent Pentecost weekend in Venice. It was incredible. It was heaven. On the Bridge of Sighs he asked me, "Are you tired, do you have any pain, do you need an aspirin?" just because I had momentarily covered my face with my hands. But that was because of my happiness. I was on the verge of weeping with joy. We had dinner in the Taverna la Fenice. I invited him, it gave me such pleasure to invite him; I also paid for the hotel, the Gabrielli-Sandwirt, naturally, because he still has to build up his Mazda dealership and besides, he has debts too, he finally admitted as much. No, he's not married. He's divorced. But I do believe he's overestimating my finances because now, ever since Venice, he wants me to move in with him in St. Pölten, he wants me to give up everything here, my office in Kremsmünster, my beautiful apartment in Steyr, my professional existence, which I have established with a great deal of effort. I am to move into his place, under the slanting walls of his bachelor pad, and help him sell Mazdas and do a bit of lawyering on the side. You have to talk me out of him. He can barely support himself with his numerous financial obligations. After we had had our first ugly fight, I thought it was over, this was the end. The next day a little electronic missive arrived: *Do not abandon me to the night, to sorrow, Dearest Love, you are my moon, O, you are my phosphorus, my candle, you are my sun, you are my light!* The words made me go soft again. How does he always manage to find the right verses? And he never mentions the author. Goethe? Ah! You think he finds them in love poetry anthologies? What I need is someone to protect me from these siren songs and tie me to the mast. I fear I can't live without him anymore. He is inside me. I have him in my blood. I am mad for his skin, his smell. He smells so good. That's why I'm now sleeping with his shirt. He wore it during our first night of love. I bury my nose in it whenever he's not with me. It intoxicates me, and his scent creates his mirage-like physical presence in me. I've already lost so much weight. I've become so skinny. I'm 5'9" and only 125 lbs. Get this! I can't wear my Armani suit any longer because the skirt is sliding down my hips. When I look at myself in the mirror, I see my skinny upper thighs. My upper thighs are much too skinny, and my rear hangs down forlornly. In skirts and jeans it's still OK, but when I'm naked it's disgusting, everything is so flabby, I hate this old skin of mine, also on my upper arms, that's why I've begun to take a daily run with my dog along the Enns embankment toward Garsten, to firm up my muscles, before I drive to Kremsmünster to my office. Wolf said my eyes were beautiful but the glasses made my face too severe. So I had myself fitted for contact lenses. They're available in all colors. I chose turquoise-colored ones. Of course I can't wear them during work and for driving I need my glasses even more, but one on one they accentuate my eyes. Sometimes my eyes burn dreadfully, but you have to be stoic, you can't just take out your lenses as you would take off your glasses. But I must admit, they produce a super effect. In special lighting my eyes look really terrific—blue-green instead of brown. They radiate like gems. I'm not exaggerating. You just have to put up with certain things. Am I stupid, or what? Not long ago a guy approached me at the gas station. "You have gorgeous eyes." I burst into loud laughter because I was thinking to myself: *Men, how easily they are deceived. A thin little layer of synthetic material, and they are smitten already.* Then he said, "You have such a lighthearted laugh, may I invite you for coffee?" Then we drank coffee together at the gas station. He thought I was a cheerful person and asked me what I was doing professionally, and I said I'm a lawyer, he couldn't believe it at all, I gave him my card, in case he ever needed help, but then he quickly took off. Since Venice everything has changed. Wolfram too has changed. Sometimes I think his personality split in Venice. Venice was heaven; Kremsmünster is hell, where messages reached me in which he insulted me. He coined his own words for these insults, he didn't require a poet for these, he scolded me in a language that was lewd and prosaic; I can't even repeat it here. What was interesting however were his suggestions that I should finally get a divorce from my asshole of a councilor, as only we called him familiarly, and he referred to Mandi, my son, as an incestuous spider monkey and so forth. All the while he made any number of spelling mistakes. Incestuous he wrote with a double s. He calls me a career-obsessed egomaniac because I'm not staying with him and supporting him in his business endeavors. He reproaches me for not wanting to give anything up for his sake. This e-mail really hurt me a great deal and I cried day and night and didn't call him anymore, I only clung to the shirt, which comforted me, his white shirt with the delicately gray dirt stains on the collar. It smells differently on the sleeves than on the collar and chest and differently still under the arms; in the back it has a different odor than in the front, but it always smells like him, and it always drives me wild. The smell of our orgasms is preserved in these textile threads, and I can sniff it out; I breathe it in, and my heart glows like a fiery hearth. I place the sleeves around my neck, I bury my face in the chest, and desire seizes me so that I almost swoon. Then I hide under the sacred garment like a wounded animal and press my craving deep inside me. Forgive me, I'm carried away, all this is not meant for strangers' ears. But then, after three endless days, another message came from him, I memorized it: *Night stealthily snatches through the folds of the curtains forgotten sunshine from your hair. Look, I want nothing but to hold your hands, to be still and kind and full of peace*. That was an apology of sorts and an offer. He wants to be still and kind and full of peace. I forgive, I forget everything, I send a reply; three words only: *I'm coming*. And I get into the car and take off and into his arms. And everything starts anew, the beautiful and the beastly. For at the end of our amorous raging is his unalterable demand: Come and stay! And when I refuse I find an e-mail the very next day disparaging me. I can't take these ups and downs anymore. I can't. He gave me another ultimatum. He doesn't realize I want only him but not his entire baggage. I can't make a new beginning, do you understand? And now I'm supposed to help sell Mazdas just because I'm crazed about a car dealer? My studies were such a struggle on top of the household, and the setting up of my legal practice, the arduous and finally successful establishment in Kremsmünster—all this I'm simply to discard for his cars? I have to give him his marching orders straightaway. You're so right, just go on. On the other hand there's something pathetic about his attachment to his cars, they're like his children, he recently explained to me. I have a child too. My Mandi, he still needs me. Almost every weekend he comes home from Innsbruck and never goes out without me. Yes, of course, it's high time for him to look for a girl. He's quite good-looking, tall, strong—gigantic actually—and on the verge of becoming fat. What am I supposed to do? A young man who only hangs around his mother, only vacations with her, that's not right. But am I to cast him out? He knows nothing about Wolfram.

Only when Mandi is out with his fraternity brothers do I let my lover come over. I want to make very distinct separations here. Days after the electronic abuse, in which I found satisfaction only with his shirt, on which his body parts, his chest, his biceps, his navel (similar to Veronica's veil) gradually began to take shape, most likely a retarded biochemical reaction to his ecstatic exhalations, I received yet another poem which I naturally fell for again. I can recite this one from memory too: *If you came, I would only need a slight resting of my hands on the young curve of your shoulder or the urging of your breasts to grow calm*. He's driving me crazy! The urging of your breasts! An entire libretto of erotic rituals suddenly clouds one's eyes and senses. I can't resist, no one can resist. I take off. I race. I return, and two days later, online, the most mean-spirited of all verbal abuses so far. I was initially startled by the thought that this obscene language could be his own: Wolfram in the original. In order to offend me he found his own words, but to dazzle my senses he borrowed from the poets. I was silent again, deeply hurt, and to stand it without him I began to drink. In the evenings before going to bed, slightly intoxicated, I wrapped myself in his shirt and had the choice of being so fired up that he only had to dream of me to feel my hot body. It was actually a miracle that I could still practice my profession under these circumstances. I had to attend a hearing. It was a case dealing with rape and subsequent death, involving several participants. We five defense attorneys sat in the courtroom. One requested the reading of the entire document, which lasted all day. And so we sat, bored, beside each other on the bench. Some of us dozed off. I had my place across from a jurist from Bad Ischl who had been called as a witness. He was my age. Days later, after we had finally lost the case, the Bad Ischl lawyer and I became better acquainted with each other. A day later I dined with him at the Steigenberger. In order to numb my longing for Wolfram, who still hadn't sent me a poetic conciliatory message, I got smashed. I think I drank a bottle and a half all by myself. I took the man home with me. From this point on, partial amnesia sets in. I know I also opened a bottle of champagne here. In any case, the empty bottle was standing on the kitchen table the following morning. And then I vaguely recall a stranger in my apartment in his underwear. Then he was lying under my cover. I also remember he tried to sleep with me and, in spite of my efforts, he did not succeed. He simply couldn't, and he didn't even apologize. All the while I wasn't even interested; he still seemed so unfamiliar, his skin, his scent. He didn't smell good. No, I didn't like his exhalations. And his nakedness was that of an old man's compared to my Wolf's. In any case we must have fallen asleep. I woke up when someone was tickling my back. *For God's sake*, I started, *there's someone in my bed!* It was very embarrassing. Then I drove him to the train station. In the afternoon already I received a message via the Internet: *Esteemed, gracious lady—May I invite you to Zauner's in Bad Ischl next Saturday?* "Gracious lady," the guy writes. This paper-pusher, this loser, this pitiful worm in pants, he makes use of the formal "you," lies naked in my bed, sits in his underwear in my apartment and uses the formal "you." And to Zauner in Bad Ischl he invites me, where all the country's retired councilor-lemurs together with their mummified wives bore each other to death, to this nursing home the style-less weakling wants to take me. No, I tell myself, I can't forget my Wolfram with this guy. In the evening when I return to the apartment, see the tousled bed, I fear the catastrophe. I search for the shirt. The shirt lies crumpled at the foot of the bed. I press my face into it. It reeks. It reeks of this impotent baboon. Not a single trace of my Adonis's scent. My sanctuary devastated, my object of satisfaction destroyed. I place it on the bed…smooth it out. I knew every shading, every yellow-brown gradation of color, every grey grain that had formed like a patina on the garment, and like a miracle—for me it was a miracle, a consecration—from one day to the next more clearly outlined his beloved body. I had possessed a true icon, a *vera icon* of my lover, this harmony of form rendered visible, which had helped me not only to solitary rapture but also to contemplative devotion. Often I knelt before the Dionysian garment, I'm not ashamed to say, and meditatively became one with the venerated body. But now his likeness was effaced, the gray, yellow, brown shades blurred, fused together; I was holding a disgusting, reeking rag in my hands which I wanted most of all to tear or cut to pieces with scissors, had I not had the crazy notion, the futile hope, that the garment, exposed to the fresh air on the balcony, would lose the stench of the paper-pusher from Bad Ischl and then the imprint of Wolfram's body would reveal itself again. On the following day I rushed to my office and went online. With a trembling click of the mouse I opened the Inbox. I stopped breathing and read: *You old cunt! Off to the crematorium with you!* Crematorium written with a "K." I don't remember what I did. I wrapped up the reeking shirt and sent it to St. Pölten. I even ran to the post office so that it would get sent that very day. Don't you agree I did the right thing? Then I suddenly felt liberated. I immersed myself for hours in my documents that were piling up like mountains since this passion had been so time-consuming. Free, I felt free. But already on the drive home, before the turn-off to Steyr, despair set in again, and alone in my apartment I got drunk until I no longer felt anything. The next day I was hung over, drove to the office, no news from him. What is the meaning of such cruelty? Help me, will you! Tell me he's a scoundrel, who will be the ruin of me, maybe he's one of those guys with a multiple personality, a Dr. Jekyll and Mr. Hyde. I'm already so skinny. When sorrow hardens with time only the body turns weak, and I'm so alone again. I forgot to tell you, my dog, my Afghan bitch, was shot by a farmer because she chased his chickens on our daily jogging route to Garsten. Well, she had a great desire to run and play, which the chickens and the farmer failed to understand. Tell me what to do now. It's a good thing you're so far away. If the people in Kremsmünster had any idea! Wait a minute. Stay on the phone. I'll quickly go online. Maybe he's written in the meantime.

5.

Battling Terror

Since I was no longer a match for Wolf's terror, I had decided to battle this terrorist with all the means at my disposal. But what were the means at my disposal? An attack would have been the worst defense in my case. No, I chose the defensive position. I let him charge my wall of silence and naturally hoped he wouldn't tire of charging it. He still literally bombarded me with telephone calls. I didn't accept his calls. I refused them steadfastly. I also did not respond to his daily e-mails. Yes, I waited for his messages, I waited for his insults, his abuse, his threats, and his declarations of love, but I no longer reacted to them. That is, I did react, but only inwardly. Frequently his messages were insolent and insulting. Then I whimpered with hurt feelings. But sometimes they were also very tender, full of rousing fantasy. He continued to come up with love lyrics and stoked my senses with them, so that I began to be inflamed at my PC and everything urged me toward him; I sat in front of the monitor and devoured his e-mails, but I didn't answer them; and this refusal offered me imperious bliss. Although I waited every day for his sweets or his whip, I imagined that our relationship was henceforth only a virtual one. In order to secure the status quo I turned to the jurist again, do you remember, the one who failed so miserably the first time? In the meantime he's become more trusting and, thanks to my efforts, somewhat more potent and in general more useful. When I lay in bed with fever and a nasty bladder infection I had to ask him for a favor. He procured the requested documents and immediately called me at noon and wanted to bring them over, make me some tea and play chess with me. The veterinarian came to mind at once, I always had to play chess with him too before he had discovered the game of solitaire on his computer; but even worse was the realization that men evidently only wanted to play chess with me because the jurist had made this request of me several times. In addition, a phone call had just come from my terrorist, and it was the first time I had become unfaithful (due to my illness-induced weakness) to my anti-terror strategy, which I had concocted in order not to endanger the virtual reality of our relationship. His voice, which I had refused to listen to for a week, brought me into a state of total dissolution, and because I still had his dark, erotically provocative tone in my ear, I simply wouldn't and couldn't play chess with the jurist, nor could I have suffered his know-it-all explanations as to which "opening moves" promised most success, since I had already opened myself completely after this telephone conversation and literally was out of my mind. And so I told the jurist to forget the chess and the tea and the dropping off of the documents because I had to go to the doctor. Then it occurred to me that my car was parked in front of the door, and should he happen to stroll by my house, it would announce my presence, and so I had to make a quick escape from the house but I really didn't know where to. And so I drove to Kremsmünster to my office and made myself comfortable on my Biedermeier chaise longue. I noticed the chaise longue still smelled like my mother's apartment, a little moldy and a little sweetish, from her perfume. Sometimes she covered herself with *Trésor* by Lancôme, I couldn't talk her out of it, it didn't become her at all, but now I poked my nose into this piece of furniture, which she had placed against my will in my office, and gradually began to relax when I suddenly heard a key turning in the lock and someone came in. It was my secretary, a moderately qualified person, who had been thrust on me by her husband, the mayor, and for business reasons I couldn't afford to reject her; she was completely flabbergasted to see me here and insisted she had forgotten her cell phone. For quite some time I had suspected her of using my office as a temporary lodging for her extramarital love life, and now I was amused by her frantic searching for her cell phone, whereby her handbag opened and the missing gadget fell out. I pretended not to see it, walked to the window and down below, in fact, stood the rural police commander, her amorous admirer, impatiently inspecting the house façade. I turned around and said: "Frau Obermayr, did you park illegally?" "Why?" she asked shakily. "Because the rural police commander is waiting for you in front of the house." She turned red as a tomato and stammered something about coincidence and rushed out of the office. I felt pretty good after this little bit of malice. But a little later my cell phone rang, it was evening meanwhile, and the jurist asked if he might still be permitted to drop off the document, he happened to be in the vicinity, he also wanted to bring me some supper and later on we could play chess. Then I became sad again, and I told him I had already been asleep and put him and his game of chess off until tomorrow. I also thought of my secretary whom I had childishly triumphed over and who was spending her amorous hours elsewhere with her police protector, but what about me? How much longer can I go on like this? Is this all? Recently the jurist picked me up for a walk. I hate going for a walk, it bores me, ever since I lost my Afghan. Yet I trotted around Steyr with the guy. He was wearing a suit, I had a suit on, and whenever we crossed a street he placed his arm protectively around me as if I were a blind chicken. I felt as if I were on an outing from the nursing home. Yet I would have needed this man so urgently to forget my terror-wolf. The other day, when I had invited the jurist for dinner at my place I asked him how he enjoyed it, and he said "Splendid" and another time "Delectable." The veterinarian used to say the same thing and it drove me crazy. And when he explained the Italian opening move to me, which he preferred to the Spanish one, he became enraptured with his monologue and failed to notice how much he bored me with it. In the mornings, when he's here, he makes the bed and it acquires a military look. He begins every sentence with: "May I?" which recently culminated in the question: "You have such beautiful shoulders. May I kiss your shoulders?" Why, I ask you, doesn't he just do it? Why is this grown man so stiff and wooden? Only now and then he dares to send me a message, so he's not so shy after all. Recently he wrote: "You envelop me like a dream." That turned me on a little. I felt like a ubiquitous aerial fairy. Another time he waltzed in with plums and apricots because I'm not eating enough fruit, and eating too little in general, and too few products containing calcium, which is necessary if you want to avoid osteoporosis, and I'm smoking too much and drinking too much. After this I was totally turned off again and returned to earth and mortality. Sometimes he talks to me as if he were my father, who by the way never talked to me like that, but I imagine a worried father talking like that to his daughter. He's only four years older than I am yet sometimes I have the feeling we have an incestuous relationship. I don't know what's the matter with me; when the guy from St. Pölten calls I'm so derailed, and every man older than 41 strikes me as a senile fool, but most likely it's me who's the fool. I'm so afraid of growing older, and sometimes in front of the mirror I look in disgust at my thighs and the area above the knee where a wrinkled bulge is beginning to form which still lets itself be smoothed out by opaque tights with 80% elasticity, but for how much longer? When Mama was still alive, I studied the aging process, the decline, on her body; I was still spared, I was too young, but after she died, a corpse from one day to the next, I felt myself exposed to aging, and I discovered that I, my body that is, was already in the midst of decline. And I panicked; everything turned topsy-turvy. I thought if I continued like this, I might as well die too. All the suppressed yearning for love and affection suddenly emerged. During the last ten to fifteen years I've come to view men as annoying troublemakers at best. But after Mama's death there awakened in me a need for affection. My body announced itself precisely at the point when I perceived its decrepitude. Tell me something sensible! Bring me to reason! If only the jurist were more appealing, everything would be easier, but not even his odor can compete with the guy from St. Pölten, I've told you already, and I have to play chess with him constantly because it gives him so much pleasure to teach me and defeat me although he lets me have the queen. And besides, I have office worries again. Business is moderate, the incoming money has slowed down, the cases are quite interesting but I can't buy anything with that. Sometimes I ask myself why I didn't become what my parents had always prophesied for me: a toilet cleaner on the Steyrer Promenade. I'd have fewer worries. Another thing is my bladder infection which I can't get rid of, I'm afraid I'm carrying resistant germs around with me that might ascend into my kidneys and I can see myself already as a dialysis patient; my coffee pot fell on my foot, it has been swollen for weeks and the doctor thinks I might have a broken toe. The doctor also diagnosed heart murmurs; but what I've learned just recently is that my abdominal aorta, yes, there is such a thing, is extremely narrowed. I wonder how the arteries in my brain are doing? I'm hellishly afraid of losing my mind. I live off my intellect. But what is the value of such an intellect if it can be totally switched off by a man's message? For example, when Wolfram's e-mail arrived announcing his intended suicide. He wanted to hang himself, he wanted to hurl himself from a church steeple in St. Pölten or from a bridge or drive his Mazda into a wall or shoot himself because he had just received the little package with his shirt, which humiliated him to such a degree and made him so desperate that he didn't want to go on living; how could I do such a thing to him. I was wondering why he hadn't mentioned the package before since I had mailed it ten days ago, but he told me later that I had written the wrong zip code on the package; an interchanged number had caused the shirt to make a detour to Vienna and the Burgenland. Naturally I reacted to my former lover's digital cry of distress. I endured his lamentations, comforted him, diverted him from his apprehensions. Finally we talked ourselves into an extreme case of longing so that I wanted to drive to St. Pölten right away, but reason, at least the tiny bit I still possess, kept me from rashness. Nor would my schedule have permitted it, so most likely it was not my reasoning powers that prevented me. But the telephone lines began to smolder, that's how often he still called, and of course I picked up every time. And every time I experienced unbounded ecstasy, rapture. People with erotic intelligence can also transport themselves verbally into ecstasy, the most extensive erotic zone is, after all, the mind, and what enters the ear, one says, arrives in the belly, and I can confirm it, until he informed me, that is until he inserted a little parenthesis in his lascivious avowals, that he was caught shoplifting. At which point I plummeted from the heights of my delights. Yes, I could actually feel my body—which had pressed toward him and opened up—shut down again, slowly cooling off and the dampness between my thighs grew cold and dried. I had a lover who was a shoplifter. A lawyer lying in bed with a criminal—what an unsavory notion! I can already see the headline in the *Kronen-Zeitung*: Female Attorney's Sex Games with Criminals (in the plural, why not?)—an unbearable thought! I gasped for air. Supposedly the day he received the package with the shirt he had been in such despair he stole a $10 video from the special-of-the-week, that is, he simply didn't pay for it, and what he took off with was *Isolde's Liebestod* with Birgit Nilsson in a Bayreuth production. It had been a compulsive act. He had wanted to slash his wrists, spill his blood to Wagnerian sounds and breathe his last. Then I realized he had acted in a state of shock: it was on account of the shirt and the unfamiliar scent clinging to it, which he noticed of course at once, and why he had flung the shirt into the garbage chute. In this unusual case I felt that the stealing of a videocassette, which was directly related to the narcissistic insult, was truly an all too understandable misconduct. And what he required now was my assistance. And yet I was steadfast enough–I'm quite proud to admit–to resist his request to represent him in the anticipated criminal proceedings. Undoubtedly more out of fear for my reputation than a rational decision. I had barely concluded the strenuous telephone conversation and his voice in my ear when suddenly the idea took hold of me that Wolfram had stolen videos before; it's been sufficiently researched that shoplifters are repeat offenders and as a rule don't get caught the first time. Surely he hadn't stolen other videos, I thought, perhaps even the CD he played when we first made love—and afterwards he sent me his shirt; he used to have innumerable little colorful lights draped along the windows and the door frame, and on the bed he spread out a soft lambskin, and then we made love to Beethoven's 6th and I remember precisely the moment when we both reached a climax during the thunderstorm…and now I can listen to the Pastorale Symphony only with tears in my eyes. And the little lights, surely he hadn't lifted those too? I was so shaken by this telephone conversation that I lost track of time; I was expected in Bad Ischl some time ago. And so after I had composed myself a little even though I had no desire whatsoever, I called the jurist and told him a story that I just made up in the course of the conversation, concocting lies while I was talking, so that I turned hot and cold at the very idea of it. I didn't simply want to call it off, because I didn't want to hurt the jurist, but on the other hand I didn't feel like seeing him either. That is my good-naturedness or my fickleness. They always get me into trouble. He believed me that my son had contracted salmonella poisoning and needed to be permanently provided with herbal tea, that his blood pressure was worrisomely low; in short, he required care and I, his mother, had to doctor him. The jurist's gullibility turned my face red with shame. But since he was still waiting for me, I decided to set out, arrived four hours late in Bad Ischl, and told him I had to leave again two hours later since I had to take care of my patient. And here I accepted the punishment for my lie: it was the first time that my inhibited jurist came out of his shell and enjoyed himself so much that he forgot our game of chess. No, don't misunderstand me, I've nothing against playing chess, there's something to the game. It's just that my time is very limited and besides, I play it all week long. Every document, every case is a game of strategy anyway; I always have to reflect on my opponent's moves before I can take tactical steps. It bores me to spend the few free hours I have playing chess. And besides, the jurist thinks I'm a pretty weak player, therefore he generously leaves me the rooks and sometimes even the queen. That's downright insulting. But the worst thing is that he praises me when I've won. Most likely he considers himself insuperable. Yet he's so messed up he always turns the light off in the bedroom. I finally told him I'd like to watch him. Then he admitted he'd always wanted to leave the light on but he assumed I'd be bashful and he didn't want to appear too demanding. As if we're dealing here with fulfillment of obligations. The annoying thing is that such an attitude makes you feel cheap. Doesn't he imply that he should be offering a payment for copulation, and since he's getting everything for free he doesn't want to ask for "more light?" What kind of an image of woman does this guy have? I mustn't even think about it, otherwise I'll go crazy. In my office, too, chaos has broken out. A so-called computer expert, a friend of my son's, installed a new system in the computer to secure the data; but the backup system has a flaw, so that all my data have now vanished. This is an irreversible defeat, and I hate not just all computer experts but also all computers. I can't wish for more. That's why I have time to chat with you at length because my work is at a standstill until an expert comes from Vienna and installs the program again. The data, however, are gone. Yes, I also remember the jurist saying he liked my pronounced facial features and he found them charming. On the one hand I was caught unawares, on the other made a fool of, but with this gesture he managed to reconcile myself at least today with my mirror image. And now I'm ashamed that I still haven't called him by his name, he's actually called Theodor. Theodor Dimitropoulos.

6.

Unexpected Reunion

I would have enjoyed going to a pub in the Old Town with Theodor. But he wanted a café, and I gave in. I was dreadfully bored with him there, and we talked about our legal documents, and then he accompanied me home. From a distance I detected a man standing at my house door. Thank God I recognized him before he could recognize me, and these two seconds sufficed for me to compose myself, because it was my beloved terrorist who was standing in front of my house. I have encountered and mastered many a precarious situation. But this was one of the more delicate ones. "You want to go in here?" I asked the person persevering at my door and belaboring the doorbell, and Wolfram answered simply with: "Yes." My heart was racing, but the jurist noticed nothing. And now I was even rewarded for lying because I knew he would go home since I had pretended that my son was still recovering from his salmonella infection at my place. He said goodbye and kissed my hand; at that moment I was grateful for his formality, and I unlocked the house door, Wolfram scurried inside and it was all over with me. Ah, dear one, I've never in my life experienced such a night of love before. And now he succeeded in winning me over. I will, after all, represent him in his criminal proceeding. I can't help myself. And of course I'm convinced meanwhile he's stolen only this one videocassette of *Tristan und Isolde*, and I'm almost ashamed of having been suspicious of him. The following morning, somewhat more sober, I explained to him that this night had been our last one, he mustn't assume we were starting over again; I was representing him only out of love for my fellow man. He had barely left when I longed for him again, yet I wanted nothing more to do with a man, any men at all, I prayed I would be strong. No, I didn't pray in a church or to any mother of God or to any Saint Anthony the Hermit. I prayed to myself. I knelt before my inner cowardice and begged: "Pity!" At the same time I felt I wouldn't be able to cope with abstinence. My Wolf had left his scent behind in my bed. His odor hovered in the bedroom and I succumbed again. After all that you can well imagine how difficult it was for me to get into the right frame of mind to see a school colleague I was to meet that evening. I couldn't come up with an excuse; for a year she's been pursuing me with an invitation to *Le Perroquet*. I had to listen to her stories, how happy she was with her husband who bestowed upon her a house and a hearth and offspring and from time to time a little necklace or a little ring. Yes, gold lures... Her husband is not an academic, she didn't study either, therefore she seems to have hang-ups and had to boast of all the things she can afford to buy. I had to keep up with her somehow because when I recently spoke to her on the telephone and mentioned ironing shirts she pointedly asked: "Whose shirts could you possibly be ironing?" And when I replied I had ironed the veterinarian's shirts for over twenty years and was still being kept busy with my son's shirts, she answered pityingly, "Well, those..." You don't count for anything unless you can iron the shirts of husbands. Since I knew I couldn't take this conversation for very long I had asked Theodor to pick me up at *Le Perroquet* at ten o'clock, which however led to his ardent desire to accompany me into my bedroom. With some effort and under the pretext I had a headache I managed to talk him out of it since I first had to air out the apartment, something I hadn't intended to do since it still smelled so deliciously of my wild Wolf. I also cried a little because he wasn't here, and I pressed the pillow covered with his scent into my face. At the same time a feeling of shame overcame me as I thought of the jurist, and tomorrow therefore as a sign of penance and absolution I shall listen with masochistic attention to his discourse on medieval humility rituals during papal coronations, and perhaps I'll ask him afterwards to turn off the light to spare him the embarrassment of lying next to me, a faithless female.

I never would have thought it possible that my power of judgment could go astray to such an extent, that I'd imagine I would grow younger just because a younger man was sleeping with me. I'm not becoming any younger just because my Wolf avoids talking about osteoporosis, doesn't bring me any fruit, and doesn't praise my wrinkles. No, I'm not becoming younger, but it's stimulating and invigorating when a younger man, instead of preaching about my eating habits, whispers already by the door how much he is longing for me, how much he desires me, and he doesn't worry about the creases on his slacks, and he doesn't demand a game of chess as foreplay nor insist on historical disquisitions or medieval papal humility rituals. Of course the jurist can't keep up with Wolf, and every encounter with my potent and imaginative lover makes me want to mock him. I realize that's very unfair, but he's so dreadfully earnest and not at all impetuous. Keep your fingers crossed that I may yet return to reason. Can one behave the way I do? What is permissible, what isn't? Actually I rather do like the jurist because he goes to great pains for me in so far as he's capable. I simply happen to make allowances and I'm too softhearted toward others, not just Theodor. The other day he ran down the Turks again, what they had done to the Greeks; I think he doesn't regard the Turks as human beings but rather as a simian species. The Greeks, he said, are simply the most attractive, with their thin noble faces. I had to laugh inwardly since he doesn't have a thin face at all. It's rather square, very angular. He also wasn't born in Greece; his parents, I believe, came to Austria in the thirties and his father managed an antique shop in Wiener Neustadt. Theodor was born here and went to school and studied here. He's an Austrian citizen. He has never lived in Greece and knows little more about it than a tourist. Still, he feels he's Greek; that's grotesque, I can't understand that at all, particularly his talk about nationality bores me, I find it such an obsolete topic today, where one talks in terms of a united Europe, a Europe without borders. He sticks obstinately to his history and points out how much the Greeks had to suffer for centuries under the Ottomans. What's amazing is that religion also plays a remarkable role in his life. I'm convinced if he lived in Greece religion would be of secondary importance, but here he supports Greek orthodoxy, even though in Bad Ischl there are only two or three true believers, no church at all, and he himself is a Catholic. Still, I could somehow get along with him, but lately he harbors thoughts of merging. He constantly obsesses about consolidating our offices; what he means of course is that

I should transfer mine from Kremsmünster to his in Bad Ischl's Kreuzplatz. No doubt he already envisions our names on one nameplate: Dr. Theodor Dimitropoulos, Jurist, and Elfriede Schweiger, Attorney. We could complement each other admirably. He could send me clients from his notary's office and vice versa. That is completely out of the question for me. For the very first time in my life–no matter how modestly–I can provide for myself and do or not do what I want. I can have one lover or five simultaneously or none, I can plan my finances according to my wishes, spend my free time according to my inclinations, read in bed night after night and simultaneously listen to Bruckner turned up high and also eat in bed any amount of chocolate at any nocturnal hour. I can leave chaos behind in the bathroom. But maybe it's time to get rid of such nasty habits. If the other person would share a little responsibility, and I'd no longer need to fear the empty apartment since someone would be there I could talk to about my day, this prospect might be rather tempting. Still, I don't want to have my arduously acquired independence taken away from me again, even though my business is worrying me right now. I really have to devote more time to my office. Besides, the jurist isn't interested in art or literature or music. All that's left for conversation is the law. And I've got that all day long anyway. And—like every man—he knows everything better. He faxes me the latest highly judicial decisions, which he highlights, and days later they then become a topic of conversation. And I'm expected to read all the imbecilities because he tests me. I have no desire to combine my career with my private life. Twelve hours with clients every day suffice. Sometimes he also strikes me as pretty absurd in his old-fashioned underwear. He's always wearing boxers. They have a libido-deadening effect on me. When I asked him, "Do you always wear this kind of underwear?" he said "Of course." Yet the other day he sat on my couch in saucy little briefs with a race car pattern, and I could barely get a hold of myself I was laughing so hard, tears were running down my cheeks and I had to make my laughing-fit plausible by telling him a joke that just occurred to me and which I had to ad lib; that is, I first had to make it up, I couldn't quite make sense of it, even the punch line escaped me, I concealed it with constant laughter, but finally he chimed in without knowing what he was laughing about. But I shouldn't be abusive because I myself have bought any amount of lingerie in St. Pölten. Ah, St. Pölten! It's come to an end between St. Pölten and Steyr. It's over. It's hellishly painful, even though I was the one who said goodbye. OK, I'll still represent Wolf, but otherwise I'll be unyielding.

7.

Jet Lag

The fact that I'm so afraid of growing old may have to do with my ambivalent professional situation. On the one hand I'm already at an age at which a woman used to be considered old, I could be a grandmother already; on the other hand, due to my late start, I'm a debutante in my profession. Particularly disadvantageous is the fact that I'm a woman. Energy is demanded of me that I can't always muster. Office worries torment me at the moment and I feel quite powerless. I should make more contacts—make myself important and visible in the public eye at festivals, Mardi Gras gatherings, and art openings. Other attorneys my age have a killer routine. For a year now there's been a second attorney in this godforsaken place, which doesn't need two. And this clever colleague happens to be a man. Men still set greater store by men. So I also have to deal with inferiority complexes, circumstances more appropriate for a young lawyer. Also being-in-love is more fitting for a young woman. Have you ever suffered from jet lag? Well, then you know how I feel…I, with the looks of a mature woman and the erotic ambitions of a young girl. What I would need is a calm, harmonious relationship—a partner to whom I can reveal my weaknesses. You can't even imagine what crazy dreams and desires I harbor lately. Suddenly it strikes me as the biggest mistake of my life not to have had a dozen children. This insane longing to hold a baby in my arms again, to smell it, to caress its soft skin... I envy young mothers with their babies, stare into their baby carriages, smile at strangers' infants and feel happy when my smile is returned. And then I realize I didn't truly experience my only child's baby stage, I don't even have any recollection of it; what did my son feel like as a baby? I've simply forgotten everything, and now it's too late and I can't make it up. But even worse than this search for lost time is my peculiar habit of analyzing every problem from countless points of view, which leads to countless divergent opinions. Of course, that's part of my daily training. I always have to take the opponents' objections into consideration. But that shouldn't result in my not taking a stance and my not knowing what opinion to have. I'm split into countless parts, sometimes I feel like a heap of rubble. How often did I end the relationship with Wolfram? But after a single telephone call or e-mail from St. Pölten I was pounded into tenderness, yes, I yearned for this being tenderized, tremblingly expected his calls, his e-mails, his invitations, his coming. These ups and downs are difficult to take, that's why I desperately need your advice. What am I to think of Theodor? I visited him yesterday in his office. He flaunted his position as boss and suddenly I was nothing more than a mere beginner, whom he had to teach the latest judicial matters. When I take a half-hour break in his office between legal and medical appointments, I want to be embraced, not instructed. But he merely pressed his thirty-page investigation entitled "The Pope's *Sedes Stercorata* as Component of the Papal Coronation Ceremony" into my hand and asked me to take it along because recently he has been researching legal-historical problems in the Roman Catholic Church, and he discovered that some historians confuse this *"sedes stercorata"* with the porphyry chairs, which likewise played or play an important role; I was supposed to quickly skim the treatise and I had to count on being quizzed during his next visit. Although this papal chair, of which I had no knowledge whatsoever, and the juridical ingenuities of my guest concerning this esoteric topic did not interest me in the slightest, yet I accepted the bundle of papers like a good girl. We didn't get home until about nine. I made us some dinner while he made himself comfortable in my living room. I'd had a very strenuous day, had to dictate legal briefs, then race to Bad Ischl, negotiate there, then to the doctor, back to the office, sign letters, buy groceries, then a consultation that lasted until long past eight—all this with a full-blown bladder infection.

I've told you, haven't I, that I'm slowly becoming incontinent. A cough, a sneeze, spontaneous laughter put me into the most embarrassing situations. Probably I'll soon have to wear Pampers. My urologist told me it was not unusual at my age for the uterus or the bladder to be dropping. That fact alone facilitates bladder infections because bacteria can readily ascend through the slack pelvic muscles. Too much hygiene was also bad because the benign bacteria are always washed away while the harmful ones stayed behind. Still, I bought special toilet paper; moist, chamomile scented. And the other day when I came home with Theodor I urgently had to go; I feared the old embarrassment would start again, and I staged an elaborate cleansing ritual and with all my wiping maneuvers with the moist towelettes I stopped up the toilet. "So much toilet paper for such a little bottom," Theodor said, and unplugged the obstruction with the plunger. I found that quite touching, but still I'm troubled by my ailment, it's an old woman's ailment, one can't deny it. My ob-gyn advised me to have electrical stimulation to strengthen my pelvic muscles; it's not supposed to be an unpleasant procedure, the opposite, actually, it's quite stimulating, costs around 500 schillings per visit. Frequent sex would also have a favorable effect on the pelvic muscles. I decided on the second option. You think I should talk to the jurist about it? Maybe it would motivate him and he'd try harder? As a precaution I constantly run to the bathroom just to make sure that the bladder is empty. And I don't even leave the house anymore without spare underwear. The reassurance of being able to change at any time protects me from the worst scenario. The other evening I went out with a girlfriend and we made fun of men and, slightly tipsy, we had to laugh so much… Later on I had to take my suit to the cleaner. That was bad, but what's worse is that on Sunday evening I poured scalding hot oil on my right leg. That must have been the councilor's revenge. I was frying a schnitzel, you see. Wiener schnitzel, which I always refused to make during my marriage, but, and I don't know why, maybe because today I'm regretting my reluctance to do him the favor, or simply because the jurist had expressed the wish for this dish and I didn't want to repeat the mistake in this relationship as in my first marriage. In any case, I promised the jurist a wiener schnitzel, and I was just in the process of frying it, when the bell rang, and I rushed to the door and greeted him, and in the middle of the greeting I remembered the schnitzel on the stove and that the heat was turned on high. I panicked that the precious scraps of meat would turn to charcoal, and so I extricated myself from my guest's embrace, ran into the kitchen and pulled the pan off the stove so violently that the hot oil spilled over and onto my foot. Assisted by my startled lover, I immediately held my foot, my entire leg, under cold water but still, a blister as big as a child's hand appeared. I ignored it just as I had resolved to ignore all blisters and bladders. The following day it burst open and I couldn't ignore it any longer; I had to go to the emergency room, received antibiotics and analgesics; it was a third degree burn, possibly a skin transplant has to be undertaken, and next week I have three to four daily hearings scheduled. How I'm going to manage that I don't know yet. In any case I'm driving home now, I'm terribly tired, I've been working too hard on the whole, and sleeping too little, and probably also drinking too much, one bottle of wine with a girlfriend and a bottle of champagne with the jurist to lessen the pain since I had forgotten my medication, and I couldn't sleep because of Mandi's tree-physiology exam; I was afraid he'd fail and then the veterinarian might possibly put a stop to his alimony payments. I've also been to the cemetery. Afterwards I bought myself a pair of Gucci jeans. Stretch. They make me look even thinner than I am. They're great. And my bottom looks small, round and firm. It must be the cut. I'm already wearing them today. Mama has been dead for a year. Her grave looks very neglected; I haven't taken decent care of the plants lately but since I'm having the gravestone erected, it wouldn't have been worthwhile.

8.

Balancing Act

Since I have to prepare for his defense I will meet with Wolf in St. Pölten in the next few days as soon as the official notification has been received by the District Attorney's office. It will, after all, only be a matter of considering an out-of-court settlement since he's already confessed to everything. Last fall after a soccer game in St. Pölten he had been involved in a brawl. Ah, my little wolf! Sometimes I call him my werewolf, which he doesn't like since he doesn't know much about Germanic mythology. Actually, he also hates his name, which his mother gave him out of animosity toward his father, who was Egyptian and a Muslim, supposedly from a well-to-do Cairo family, and who left her when she became pregnant. In any case, he suddenly had vanished, and his mother, blond and blue-eyed, had to explain to her ultra-Catholic family that her dark-haired and dark-eyed son quite apparently did not have a father from the Alpine region. Nonetheless, or precisely for that reason, she gave him the name Wolfram and had her dark-locked son baptized and raised as a Catholic, with the result that at twenty he converted to Islam and ten years later returned to Catholicism. This inconstancy, this indecisiveness is a typical trait in Wolf, and sometimes I feel we are soul mates. I've discovered something else we have in common. He too was abandoned by his father. Of course his problem is different since Wolfram never even had a chance of becoming acquainted with his procreator, nor is it permitted that he be mentioned in the family. Wolf doesn't even know his name—he is said to have been a resident physician in the St. Pölten regional hospital and his mother was a nurse there—whereas I, on the other hand, was tormented by my father until the age of nineteen. That no longer troubles me, since I could get even with him; I no longer hold a grudge. But Wolfram had no chance at all to have it out with his procreator. He had only his mother, and he seemed to have taken it out on her from time to time. These complicated circumstances contributed to his ambivalent character. Sometimes he's wild, then gentle, sometimes courageous, then cowardly, worried and carefree. In any case he rescued me from my virtually desiccated existence. On his guitar he performed chansons for me; in his free time he plays the tuba with the St. Pölten Brass Band; we have the same taste in music, and for the first time in my life I had the impression that a man valued my opinion, and besides he constantly told me how clever I was. At least that's how it was in the beginning. *One* advantage to living with him would be that no legal documents would appear on my night table since he has rather anarchic relations with rules and laws. I realize I'm involuntarily drifting into pleading his case. I only wanted to vent my annoyance and suffering, for my Wolf, my wild animal, this erotomaniac, is sometimes very hurtful and cruel. I was just smoking a cigarette and relaxing in the hallway during a break in the proceedings in the Steyr Provincial Court when my cell phone went off and the brute informed me of the fact of his executed coitus with his ex-wife, that he realized there was no going back to her. And he thinks I'd be happy about the news. Of course in moments of rage, I must admit, I urged him several times to give his ex another try, but in reality I thought he'd be physically incapable of copulating with any woman other than me. The erotic experiences with me, I secretly hoped in my delusions of grandeur, would have made him immune to every other woman, therefore the very idea that he's sleeping with his ex almost made me lose my mind. And now I'm sitting here and weeping. Surely he's not doing with her what he's doing with me? Whispering the same lunacies into her ear? I want nothing more than for him to be here so that I can smell him. Still, I have a bad conscience because of my relationship with Theodor; just imagine, recently he told me I had such a spacious soul and he was envious of it; I was touched and embarrassed because it's so spacious that, yes, two men simultaneously have enough room in it. Should I change? Sometimes I try to convince myself that the jurist is more suitable for me. He is punctual and waits patiently. I think he generally likes to wait, and in particular for me. There's something of a confirmed bachelor about the jurist that I find extremely provocative. It gives me pleasure to see how much I can lure out of this spinsterish jurist with all my dexterities; it's like kneading dough: something comes into existence and grows. On the other hand, he gets on my nerves with his suggestions: how I should adjust the thermostats in my apartment to save energy, but he forgets I like to have it warm and I'm prepared to pay for it. He also wants to advise me on the purchase of a new bed, that is, he wants to meddle and ultimately control me. Recently he even explained to me his intellect told him there was no such thing as lasting love and therefore he was always asking himself over and over whether he could trust his emotions. What does this paper-pusher and document-stamper expect after such an admission? I coldly explained to him he should trust only his intellect since his emotional life at any rate was underdeveloped. Now he's whimpering a little and going head over heels with obliging offers: May I please…etc.; I strictly decline everything. He invited me to dinner for tomorrow evening—but I'm keeping him dangling and justifying it with my medications, which I have to take because of my wiener-schnitzel-burns, and which medicine, in any case, suppresses my appetite. On the weekend I have to care for my son again; the pile of laundry to be ironed is five feet tall. I'll be listening to Mandi who's now the press reporter for the action committee in the Austrian University Student Association and he has written several good contributions opposing the introduction of tuition; therefore I'm now intensely involved with media law to protect him. I prefer it a thousand times that Mandi is taking an interest in the action committee instead of constantly running to his fraternity. I simply can't stand these Pharisees. I'm particularly proud of having rescued him from their clutches. However, I'm still worried about Mandi because he still doesn't have a girl. The other day the veterinarian called me; he seems to be a little jealous, he asked to have a talk with me, and on the telephone he indicated that his relationship with his girlfriend, whom he had met a year after our separation, had cooled off and he was often very, very lonely. On this occasion I reminded him again of our son's inhibitions and I made the suggestion that he take Mandi to a cathouse so that he'd finally learn to enjoy his sexuality. The veterinarian produced only inarticulate sounds of refusal and declared he'd not go to any cathouse. Fine, I can't be in charge of everything. Yes, certainly, my son needed a more mature woman who'd introduce him nurturingly to the world of eroticism, a sex teacher, because, to be honest, if I were the young girl, I wouldn't be turned on by Mandi either. He's OK in a suit, but without clothes? He's simply too fat. I've told him, "Mandi, you have to exercise, run, or swim." But he has no perseverance. Should I find him a wife perhaps, maybe through an ad?

9.

Lust and Frustration

I succeeded in having Wolfram's shoplifting case pending in the District Attorney's office dismissed on its merits. The District Attorney knew of course that a female attorney was involved in the case in more ways than one. As a rule, that calls for objections, appeals, a lengthy proceeding, motions to receive evidence, etc., and all on account of a videocassette valued at one hundred fifty schillings. In that case they'd rather dismiss than carry out such a complicated ceremony because of a triviality. Wolfram now considers me Central Europe's best defense attorney. Ever since he received the written notification that his case was dismissed he can barely contain his enthusiasm for me: I'm the most terrific woman of his life, and his life's dream, pure and simple. An attorney like me can hold her own anywhere, in particular in the provincial capital St. Pölten, which would be a much more fitting place for me than Kremsmünster. I'm much too attractive, too sexy, too clever, too well read, too educated, too warmhearted, too sweet, too exciting, what a pity therefore to go to waste in this godforsaken place. No,

I really do not want to go to waste here, but the cafés and restaurants I'd have at my disposal in St. Pölten (it's lunch break here at the moment) aren't particularly overwhelming either. St. Pölten, he exclaimed, was waiting for an attorney like me. And he can already see me strolling down the shopping avenue, trying on suits and chic dresses in the boutiques, going out to eat, and he's whispering into my ear passionate confessions that he remembers the exciting hours with me and his heart is beating wildly and God knows what else…and then I have to get a good grip on myself not to lock up the office right then and there and race to St. Pölten. But yesterday my Wolf made a surprise appearance; I had to cancel the jurist at once saying I still had to draft some documents. He pitied me that I had to work so hard, and I felt a bit embarrassed. But not for very long because then I lay in the arms of my werewolf and felt rescued and taken care of. We celebrated my triumph over justice the entire night. Wolfram said when I'm lying in his arms I look like a young girl. I thanked him for the compliment but didn't tell him about the role gravity plays in these circumstances; everybody knows that gravity pulls the fatty tissue down, and thus smoothes the wrinkles and tightens the skin. This phenomenon manifests itself impressively with the dead. Have you ever seen a freshly deceased person that's wrinkled?

My dead mother looked as if she'd gotten a facelift. After a certain age one should only be observed in a recumbent position, a supine position, mind you; a side view is as problematic while standing as while sitting. In lying on your side, however, the cushions of fat and wrinkles shift to one side and form into a clump; one side of the face is hollowed out and even looks bony, the other side is wobbly with too many layers of skin. Above all, don't lower your face and look down on the man; that'll age you by ten years because gravity in this case allows the slack cheeks to dangle toward the observer like pouches, especially the wrinkles around the mouth and eyes are emphasized. Tear sacs, which vanish if you're lying on your back, turn into thick bulges. A woman has to know this. But I'll take care not to deprive Wolf of his illusions. Actually I intended to bid him a final farewell after the proceedings were over: I had informed him of my intention. But on the morning after this sleepless night I had neither the time nor the strength for it; he already had to leave for St. Pölten at six and I at eight for Steyr to a hearing. And so we had no choice but to hurriedly drink some coffee together and smoke a cigarette; my thoughts had already turned to my court hearing, and his, most likely, to cars. Did I tell you he's designing a homepage for me? He can do that too. That's important for business. I'll have to come up with all sorts of images pertaining to my person: all modesty and restraint which, in any case, would be inappropriate for the internet, must be discarded, and I'll portray myself as a top attorney. Wolfram wants to show me in full figure from head to toe and in motion, once from behind in Gucci jeans to show off my athleticism, dynamism, and youthfulness; and from the front in my Armani suit, which is to emphasize my efficiency, competence, and intellectual side.

After the court hearing I had to rush home, shower, wash my hair. Then at eleven thirty a meeting to discuss the evidentiary court order. Then back to Kremsmünster to read my mail.

10.

Symbioses

I was looking forward to the weekend with my son. On Saturday I did the laundry and cooked meals for him which he takes back to Innsbruck in tight containers and then only has to heat up in his apartment so that he doesn't have to eat in the student cafeteria since he dislikes the food there, and on Sunday I ironed his shirts. He always pressured me to be ready with everything by five since he usually wanted to leave by then. But this time he seemed in no hurry to depart although I had gotten everything ready. When I asked him when he was thinking of leaving, he said he was staying on. I took a deep breath and told him that didn't suit me at all since I was expecting a visitor. My son then made a real scene, which distinguished itself in no way from that of a jealous lover's. He became almost histrionic, even a bit shrill. He never expected any gratitude once he'd served his purpose, he raged. For years he had suited me fine, he had to comfort and console me; he reminded me of all the scenes in which he had seen me weak and bathed in tears, and that's true, there were quite a few. Supposedly I had burdened and bothered him with my office worries, patiently he had confronted even my most ridiculous little complaints. I should ask myself what I would have done without him after grandmother's death, he said in a voice betraying emotion. As far as he's concerned he renounced contacts with friends for my sake, and now I was throwing him out of the house because of my men. I immediately had a bad conscience, tried to be conciliatory and told him I was willing to uninvite my guest whom I was expecting at eight. I reached for the cell phone, dialed Theodor's number, whereupon my son tore the gadget out of my hand. Suddenly, I was still fighting with my Mandi when the text message appeared informing me that he, Theodor, wasn't coming, after all, until Monday, if that was agreeable to me. I thought the jurist had suddenly developed divinatory talents, and I sent him a message that in fact it would suit me better. And so Mandi stayed on although I was still mad at him for some time. On the next day when I called Theodor I found out that my call had reached him and he had heard our argument. Of course I felt extremely embarrassed since I still refer aloofly to Theodor as the jurist whenever I'm speaking to Mandi in order to stoke his jealousy. I also felt awkward when I learned that Theodor was of the opinion I had let him overhear on purpose to call for his help. Lately I fall from one embarrassment into another. Something's wrong; I'm always feeling ashamed or I am being shamed. That weakens my position toward my partners. And so I had to make special efforts to appease Theodor, who was a bit put off at first and reluctant to tell me how much he had overheard, and instead he told me that on Saturday he had attended a colleague's birthday party. He would have been so happy had I been there because I would have been the princess, so young and still so beautiful. I was his Snow White because with my black hair, white skin, and red mouth I looked like her; I had something delicate, something ethereal. I was rather pleased by that. But recently he sent me a text message with the following content: *kittysweetieeeee…xoxo.* At first I had difficulty deciphering the message. I tried strenuously to figure out the meaning of the message when Mandi, who happened to be here and was looking over my shoulder, burst out laughing and roared: "Kittysweetieeeee! My mother's lover writes kittysweetieeeee with five E's!" He slapped his thigh and could barely contain his amusement. I was really furious at the jurist who, before the whole world, is denigrating our relationship to a kindergarten level. In any case his messages continue: "Have you gone beddie-bye?" Sometimes I ask myself what I'm dealing with. Is this a grown man? Or is he perhaps a latent pedophile, as Mandi recently presumed, who is verbally at least living out his longings? If only the jurist knew how unerotic he strikes me with these verbal diminutions! Not long ago I attended the furniture fair in Wels with him. I'm still sleeping on a mattress since my bed deliveryman did not make his promised delivery for months, and I cancelled the contract. I wanted to look for a compatible bedstead. Waterbeds are very much in vogue now and I tried one out. But my companion virtually panicked because he fears that "some things" may no longer be possible in a "waterbeddie." He's worried evidently about our balance and that our amorous games on the "waterbeddie" could get out of hand and turn into a wild, uncontrollable tumbling about. Therefore he insistently urged me to distance myself from the acquisition of such an unstable place of repose. As you see, he meddles already in all sorts of things, and I'm on the brink of losing autonomy in my own household. Besides, he also acts very indiscreetly, if not compromisingly, in public. It's simply not possible to walk beside him without being touched somewhere, held, taken, or seized by my hand. Half the town has seen us strolling intimately like that. Even in the monastery church in Kremsmünster in the evening during a big organ concert he had to place his arm around me because he feared I was getting too cold. But

I wasn't cold. In any case he has a cold now. Here, too, we were observed by colleagues and some of my clients. After a hearing he picked me up for lunch and on the steps of the courthouse he placed his arm around my shoulders for the whole world to see. Yes, I've often complained to you about his stiffness and formality, but this placing his arm around and about me is nothing spontaneous; just the opposite, it's conventional and solicitous. Moreover, with his touching he makes me his possession, like a dog that marks his territory with his urine. I should seriously forbid him such behavior, but most likely it would hurt him. I don't want to do that either. That's precisely the crux. I want to please everyone. Maybe that's why I became a lawyer. I can't even stand up to my son, my quasi-super husband. How often did I take advantage of him as my heart's consoler? How am I supposed to free myself from this symbiotic relationship? I've always thought of myself as the best of all possible mothers. And now I'm supposed to have done everything wrong? It's his father—the councilor and veterinarian—who is at fault; he's the one who withdrew from everything, dispatching only advice, instructions, yes, orders from his hellhole in Mühlviertel. But he was not capable of delivering visual aids to Mandi, suggestions how to deal with women, how to approach the opposite sex. I'm as convinced as ever that it's his responsibility to find a girl or a mature woman for him. There's a saying from Flaubert: if he'd ever had a son it would have been a great pleasure for him to provide women for him. But the councilor is no poet and even less of a genius. He considers it an unreasonable demand. Surely there must be women in his office that would be suitable for his son's defloration. She could be a married woman, an erotically experienced but sexually frustrated civil servant, an employee, a secretary or a case worker would be ideal, one who could do Mandi as well as herself a good turn. Wouldn't that be a nice assignment for any woman, in particular for a mature woman? I wouldn't pass it up. But in this case as a mother my hands are tied. Besides I really can't take charge of everything. I'm now preparing for a three-day lecture series dealing with media and information competence in which I'll take part in two weeks. No, I can't be more specific, but doesn't it sound quite interesting? It takes place at a conference site in St. Pölten. Wolf wants to come too. And so I'm already wondering how to stage my appearance there, not at the conference but my confrontation with Wolfram. Should I proudly refuse to see him and go to the hotel? I broke off with him, didn't I? In any case, I announced my intention. And what am I to tell Theodor? Should I even say anything? What if he wants to accompany me to this seminar? These are problems I love to occupy myself with to fuel my anticipation. I'll buy myself a great dress and maybe get a new hairdo. But once again my conscience is tormenting me because of my two other men. Actually I want all three.

11.

Physical Resistance

My attendance at the lecture series almost didn't come off at the last moment because the jurist didn't leave my side, hovered near me every evening, and it seemed as if his daily appearance would turn into a regular habit. The relatively long drive from Bad Ischl to Steyr also couldn't keep him away. All my nervousness made my cold worse and it wasn't until I pulled the thermometer out from under my armpit and showed him that my fever had climbed to 100 that he conceded I had to cure myself and he too might be endangered if he stayed on. And so, even though a day later than planned, I could finally depart. This was the fifth infection I had to cure during the last six months. It all started in May. After Venice I was already struggling with bronchitis and had to interrupt my telephone calls because of my coughing fits. Sometimes I thought I'd suffocate during one of these attacks. Three times, back-to-back, I suffered from bladder infections that threatened to affect my kidneys. I realize all my bladder infections started after I met the jurist. Sometimes I think even his bacteria are incompatible with my body.

Then came the infected wound from the schnitzel burn, likewise ascending into blood poisoning. Now it seems another bronchitis is developing from a harmless cold. It's a known fact that stress lowers one's immune resistance, and during the past few years I've been stumbling from one stressful situation into another. Still, I wanted to go to St. Pölten. I was so excited, high spirits bordering on pain, and my heart was racing; the idea of finally seeing Wolfram again put me in a mighty euphoric mood. All my good intentions of farewell and separation were forgotten. I wanted to let myself fall into his arms, forget myself completely, and experience a flight to heaven. But things began immediately with a small disappointment. Already on the telephone, Wolfram unexpectedly explained that he did not want to accompany me to my seminar after all. It was too media-oriented, and therefore of no interest to him. At that point, I would have been willing to drop the whole event, but he said he wanted to pick me up from the conference. I left the seminar room a few minutes before the session ended to freshen my makeup and then quickly headed for the exit of the seminar building, where I waited for him as we had arranged. I was terribly nervous. I began to freeze in my light, elegant shoes. I smoked one cigarette after the other. Finally, he appeared half an hour late. In the darkness and wearing my contact lenses, with which I can't see into the distance, I didn't recognize him until the very last moment. Suddenly, he stood before me in a washed-out polo shirt and sweatshirt. And I was waiting for him in my very best outfit. I wore my pink Escada suit for the first time. I had bought it just for this occasion, and it transformed me completely. Underneath, I was wearing my newest sexy lingerie. And I had gone to a clever hairdresser who had constructed a smashing look with my hair swept up on my head, and she had conjured a reddish shine into my black hair. And here I was, waiting in the dark, pacing back and forth to stay warm, and failed to see him approaching. He simply stood before me as if suddenly produced by magic and said "Hi!" Simply Hi! I had expected him to embrace me impetuously and lift me up, as he always did when he greeted me, and whirl me around. But he only said "Hi," and placed his languid arm around my waist. Then we went to a very average, virtually empty restaurant. A more elegant one would have been out of the question because of his getup. And then the cold that I first felt in my legs crept up into my chest. Have you ever felt anything like it? Something icy, which emerges from within and strangles every warm emotion? At first, words failed me. Then the electrically charged sparks that usually flew between us vanished, not even a tiny erotic sparkle stirred within me. I no longer knew what to say to him; I searched for a topic, for something stimulating, something that concerned us both, but nothing occurred to me. He too was pretty monosyllabic. We ordered our meal. My pork cutlet was dry and tough. In my despair I drank quite a lot of wine, a very average Zweigelt. And still this man displeased me more and more. I asked myself what I had ever seen in him; his nose, his mouth, his black locks repulsed me, and even his smell, which had driven me crazy, bothered me. Suddenly an abyss had opened up between us, between me, well groomed, elegantly and expensively attired, and him; the man sitting beside me looking like a tramp in his dirty polo shirt and his polyester pullover from C&A. I had put on my grandmother's pearl necklace, the matching earrings, my emerald ring inherited from my mother. I exuded Calvin Klein's *Obsession*, our favorite perfume. In the restaurant's mirror I could see myself: enchanting, downright bewitching. You can visualize it, can't you? It's amazing how externals become significant at certain moments. I was ready to go to bed with myself—that's how much I liked myself—but not with the man who evidently hadn't even taken a shower before he came. Of course after dinner he suggested we go home to his place. Although I was tired and drunk I rejected his offer because I had the feeling of degrading myself in this misalliance. He tried to persuade me, became louder and louder, our voices echoed in the dark street; he shouted, I shouted back, as I've said I was already drunk, and it gave me more than a little pleasure to resist his brutal pressure. After a violent scene in the parking lot I jumped into the car and stepped on the gas. He staggered back, and that gave me an intoxicating feeling of power. But now it was midnight and the idea of having to drive back more than sixty miles made me realize how tired I was, and suddenly I wasn't sure any longer if it was a triumph or if I should have chosen the soft bed instead of the autobahn. I was afraid of falling asleep while driving and being crushed by one of the gigantic trucks that were wedging me in. At the last minute I steered toward an autobahn rest stop where quite a few trucks were already parked. In a remote corner, next to some tall shrubbery, I parked my car, lowered the backrest, wrapped myself in a warm cover, turned on a CD which happened to be Beethoven's Sixth which evoked painful memories and brought tears to my eyes, but finally lulled me to sleep. At five I woke up shivering with cold and urgently had to go to the toilet. But it was still dark outside and I was so cold and afraid to leave the car, my protective steel shell, and so I drove off and turned on the heat to make myself more comfortable, if only there hadn't been this distressing urge to urinate. I began to sing loudly to calm myself, but instead I fell into a coughing fit against which my bladder could not hold its own. I arrived at home smelly and wet. The repulsive wetness had penetrated even into my shoes. Thank God my car has vinyl leather seats, but my suit had absorbed everything like blotting paper, likewise the carpet, which I threw at once into the garbage. I immediately took a relaxing bath with lavender fragrance, and while the warm water was embracing me, I came to an understanding with myself. As I was hanging my new suit on the balcony to dry, I was wondering to which cleaners I should take the odiferous piece of clothing. It had to be on the other side of town where no one knew me. I flung my lace lingerie immediately into the washing machine. *Now*, I thought, *it's over, finally over, that's what I've always wanted–he no longer means anything to me*. But soon the next frustration set in. Since I was now unexpectedly spending the weekend alone, I remembered Theo and called him up, telling him I was cured meanwhile and suggesting he should visit an art opening with me on Sunday. To my surprise, he turned me down. He already had plans. At the same time he reproached me for not having answered his text message yesterday, which read: *bunny, bunny*. Am I supposed to reply to such a message? What is one to say to bunny, bunny? I'm not going to let myself sink to that level. And so I thought, why should I hold on to the jurist when I said goodbye to the guy from St. Pölten. And so I insisted on *tabula rasa* and announced to him that I'd furl the flags he hoisted in my apartment and send them to him in a package. Then I hung up. You have to realize that he had recently deposited his bathrobe as well as his warm-up suit at my place and thus tried to occupy more and more territory in my apartment. Lately he took to wearing one of those grotesque fedora hats in a hideous plaid. He looked like Dick Tracy, that caricature of a detective from an old comic strip, do you remember? The square, protruding chin, the narrow, clenched mouth. Utterly ridiculous! At the door already I could barely contain my laughter. He had hardly entered the apartment when he removed his tie, then his suit: a plaid cap and a suit! This man is nothing but a breach of style. He took it off, made sure the creases in his trousers were aligned, placed the jacket on a hanger, and then slipped into his warm-up suit, which he had left at my place. I hate warm-up suits. The veterinarian always wore them too. Then they lounge about, these masters of creation, in front of the TV and !ook like monkeys. And I've conformed to this jurist in every way. Even in Fuschl I went for a stroll with him, walking up the esplanade to the castle and back. He, the all-important gentleman, his left hand casually in his trouser pocket, and with his right one he clung to me. From time to time he made a sweeping gesture toward the scenery, pointing to the lake, as if he were the lord and master of this land. In the evenings, back in my apartment, he never lifted a finger but sat in his baboon-butt-colored (purple, orange and green) warm-up suit on my couch in front of my TV, sat down at the set table like a husband and just like a husband began to criticize me: I was watching too little TV. I should at least watch the news. That was part of one's education, and in general I wasn't reading the newspaper enough. That did it for me. I don't have domestic help as he does, you see. What was this man actually accomplishing? Even sexually I had to serve him. I had to seduce him, otherwise nothing at all happened. I'm not saying it wasn't fun for me occasionally. It was time and again a minor success to transform a flaccid bag of skin into something taut and useful, but not always. In order to avoid routine and tedium I had to come up with new ideas and I always did manage to be inspired. But the fact that I also had to take care of him, provide him with alcohol—he even smoked my cigarettes—all that got on my nerves. I'm happy I put an end to this episode, finally: no more ecclesiastical-legal excursions, no longer the eternal lamentations against the Turks, I was finally permitted to crawl into my bed alone, spread out, read and turn up the music as loud as I wished, and above all listen to what I wanted to listen to. In the meantime I've found out he has quite a few financial worries, therefore he wanted to convince me to consolidate our offices and enter upon a so-called life partnership–without a marriage certificate naturally. That's over. But the vexation goes on. A client was not in agreement with the outline of my grievance. I tried to explain to him in vain that the grievance merely must state the narrative of the grievance. He was incapable of understanding why I wasn't permitted to operate with *verba legalia* nor the circumstance that I didn't have to point out to the court the corresponding paragraph from the law, for otherwise it might have felt toyed with in such an unequivocal legal situation. I felt so down I would have liked nothing better than to cast everything aside. But what else was there? That's the question. And today my rejected Wolf cried into the phone again. He felt terrible. His depressions had taken over again. My God, I was thinking, what about my depressions? I'm not humanity's consoler; I could use some consolation and recognition myself, a shoulder to cry on. And if my son wouldn't let himself be misused from time to time, there'd be no one here for me. Men only want to go to bed with me. I'm not wholly lacking in talent there. No, all this had to end, even at the risk of having to resort to a stimulating gadget. But then the jurist announced himself again. You'll never guess how! A text message: *sweetiebunny so alone!* It was followed by a phone invitation to a country inn for next Sunday. He'd sooner lead a camel through the eye of a needle than "sweetiebunny" to a country inn, I told him, and he'd better look for a fool to accompany him. He should look for a woman with imagination to compensate for his lacking one. Then he acted totally crushed. He knew he had hurt me because he didn't want to go with me to the art opening, but–he was so wretchedly sick, he was suffering as much as ever from bronchitis and he couldn't admit that to me because he didn't want to become a victim of my pitilessness. My strength in general tended to make him nervous. And lastly, my cough was still worse than his and he had wanted to avoid re-infecting himself. Yesterday he even had to take an aspirin. He hated pills, in fact he even had a horror of them, but that's how bad it was, his headaches especially. There was only one possibility to become healthy again and that was the self-imposed quarantine. I told him I needed a man, not a delicate little creature who is driven crazy by an ordinary banal infection which thousands upon thousands catch every spring and fall. The funny thing is that he infected *me* with *his* cough. Well, that's what happened. And now this man accuses me of pitilessness! That's just going too far. Unfortunately I have way too much pity for the whole world, but a common cough doesn't set it in motion. Every day we move about in our workplaces in badly ventilated courtrooms and magistrates' offices, no wonder if one catches an infection. The jurist reminds me yet again of the veterinarian. He used to wrap a warm scarf around his neck at home in the fall and didn't take it off again until early summer. He walked about the apartment with a woebegone look and pampered his sore throat. I had to serve vast quantities of herbal tea, bring him the thermometer and then withdraw so as not to disturb the invalid. And this jurist maintained he was afraid of me! I'm not strong at all, that's why I'm playing the role of a strong woman, otherwise I'd be a pushover in this male domain that the field of law still is. And now he even fears my cough, which I caught from him! What is this guy doing in court? What if someone coughs on him? I'm of the opinion: either your physical resistance works or it doesn't work. It was easy for me to let him go.

12.

My Hands Tied

I won a legal aid case on appeal. The verdict came in today. I was awarded 350,000 schillings in compensation. I skipped and hopped through the office! In a written brief my opponent had charged me with a critique of capitalism tinged with Marxism. I succeeded then in transferring this matter from the commercial court to the welfare court. There they sided with me. My adversary, he happened to be a lawyer from St. Pölten, was so infuriated by me, he never acknowledged me with a glance, let alone a greeting, before the individual hearings of which there were six. Out of sheer fury he evidently lost his mind during the appeal. It was not executed according to the law. The Court of Appeals followed every point of my argumentation, as the verdict indicates. That was reason to rejoice, and now I could hold my head high again. The same day that I received the news of my court victory, which suspended my office worries for the time being, I had a surprise visitor in my apartment. The doorbell rang and when I opened, Wolfram stood before me. He had brought me *Obsession* as well as food and drink. I was lucky in that I had already stowed away Theo's bathrobe, his warm-up suit and his house shoes, even though I hadn't mailed the stuff yet because of lack of time. Wolf was lamenting: the reason he had been so unresponsive and depressed that time was because I had threatened him with separation; the botched evening was entirely my fault. But he couldn't be without me any longer, and so he showed up here. I felt as if the heavens had opened up again. I couldn't help but embrace him, laughing and crying at the same time. I felt great again. Can you understand that? I allowed myself to feel great again, that everything was fine. But two days later I was waiting for him in vain. I had put some champagne on ice and CDs in the player, I had arranged candles I was going to light, prepared little sandwiches; I wanted to present myself fragrant and in a skintight Wolford outfit with a tiger look. I waited. It became colder and colder, even though I had turned the heat up high. Finally around eight the doorbell rang in my office. I jumped up. I was surprised however that he simply didn't come in, rush in. After all he was two hours late. How quickly I melted, how warm I suddenly felt! I tore open the door and recoiled because before me stood the elementary school principal, who had taken early retirement and for whom I had once won a damage suit, and he said he'd been watching me for a long time and noticed how often I had been working late into the night at the office; so much work is not good for such a beautiful young woman (yet he's my age, in his early fifties, but retired for health reasons) and he asked whether he might come in for a moment. He pushed me aside before I could say anything and closed the door behind him. He had a peculiar spark in his eyes and I thought to myself I mustn't provoke him and said I was just in the process of leaving, but if there was something on his mind he should tell me. Yes, there was something on his mind; he explained bluntly that he loved me, was dreaming of me every night, and he came closer and closer, his bad breath struck my face; I took a step back, then another, which was not the wisest thing to do because I was suddenly pushed into a narrow place, jammed in between the chaise longue and the strong body of this man, his protruding belly and his strong chest pressed toward me. He had seized my hands and wanted to push me with the weight of his body onto the couch. "Leave me alone," I screamed, and whatever else one shouts in a situation like this. I threw my head back and forth because this fellow wanted to press his fat lips on my face. "But, beautiful lady, I'm not doing you any harm," he said. I knew his left hand was weakened ever since his stroke and he wouldn't be able to hold me for long in his scissor grip. Finally, I freed my right hand and I reached out to slap him hard, once, then twice. The slaps hit home; the palm of my hand was burning. I was nauseated by the skin and soft cheeks of the strange face, as if by unwanted intimacy. My resistance bewildered him to such a degree that he also let go of my other hand and I was able to push him out of the office. I fell back upon the cushioned bench and began to weep with rage and humiliation. I can't even turn him in, I'd become the object of ridicule in the whole town; people would laugh themselves silly if they learned of the episode, and besides, I'd have a problem proving it. I wasn't injured, no traces of violence on my body, not a bruise as circumstantial evidence of an attack, I had experienced an insult but de facto nothing had happened to me. It was my lover, however, who had to be held responsible for my fright and insult, for had he come his presence alone would have protected me from the desires of the deranged pedagogue. It's definitely over now. I've felt it last week already, but when he showed up again, I was overwhelmed by his temperament, his impulsiveness, and now he paid me back.

13.

A Sunday Outing

Since it's definitely over with St. Pölten, I accepted Theodor's invitation to a Sunday outing to Salzburg. In any case it was a nice change for once not to drive to Gmunden or Bad Ischl but to Salzburg instead, to a city that the entire world likes. But on a Sunday in late November nothing was happening there either. It was gloomy and cold, we were strolling in the Getreidegasse, and I saw the many elegant shops which did me no good since they were all closed; some, the jewelry stores, were even barred. Once again a feeling of panic arose in me that I was wasting my time here, at his side, and I told myself I would never again drive to Salzburg on a Sunday, where I couldn't do anything after a walk but go to Café Tomaselli, read a newspaper and drink a large latte. I didn't need the Tomaselli for that, I can do the same in Steyr, where the waiters greet me as "Frau Magister" and show me immediately to a window seat, but here no one knows me, and only Americans at best have status, and we had to take a seat at a tiny drafty table. Sitting at a little table in a corner has depressed me since my childhood. Too often my parents, in particular my councilor-father, had banished me from the parental table to the low corner table. I used to sit there, at the low little table that was much too low, and bend over my food. Secretly I reproached my companion for not having protected me, or not being able to protect me, from the little corner table at the Tomaselli. In Salzburg, he was as much of a zero as I was: a nobody, whereas in Steyr and Kremsmünster's trendier places I had status. At the far end of the Getreidegasse a little shop was open after all; it displayed artistically pretentious Christmas tree ornaments, and I stopped in front of it because everything else bored me and because I discovered some light behind the shop window, something human, something warm, while I had become cold under my mink coat from looking at the brightly lit boutiques that displayed beauty I could neither touch nor try on since everything was shut down as if dead. I believe we were the only ones strolling through the Getreidegasse on this gloomy November Sunday, at least we were one of the very few, and so I spontaneously stopped in front of the shop window with the glittering glass bulbs and the arts and crafts gold angels from Rausche, and Theo asked me would I like something, and I said yes, although I really can't stand Christmas tree ornaments and Rausche gold angels and especially not Christmas trees, and we entered the shop. I chose two of the gold angels, the cheaper ones, because I didn't want Theodor to spend so much money for something that didn't mean anything at all to me; actually I only wanted to give him the opportunity for a friendly gesture, to allow him a gesture of generosity. I had the two glittering angels wrapped up, the woman wrote out the bill, it amounted to 600 schillings and I glanced about for my companion who wanted to settle the bill, but he was already standing at the door, doorknob in hand. I must have misunderstood him and so I paid the bill. Now I had to carry the angels in a ridiculous plastic bag because they didn't fit into my purse. When my companion asked whether he might help me carry something, perhaps the angels, I began to laugh; I laughed loudly and for a long time, and this laughter liberated me and confused him, and I pressed the little bag with the angels into his hand and I thought we were both ridiculous.

On the drive home I turned the conversation to us. I was in an aggressive mood. I wanted to lure something out of him, wanted to hurt him with something, and I was searching for a vulnerable spot into which I could drive my caustic tongue. In the apartment I continued to bellyache, I reproached him with lacking in trust and lacking in affection, just so, it just occurred to me, and he began to defend himself somewhat. I didn't listen to him, but I observed him; he suddenly struck me as lively, spontaneous, and I thought of my St. Pölten lover with whom it was definitely over now, and I thought: *Maybe I can still do something with the jurist after all, something beyond the post-infantile or pre-senile "elfisweetie, beddiebye?" and "such a cute little behind" text message, something grown-up*, and his eyes flashed at me as they otherwise only did when he was lecturing on the Greek history of suffering. His mouth made me long to kiss him and so I began to become active and get him to be silent and act. We succeeded indeed in having breathtaking coitus with a considerable orgasm. But as Virgil, I believe, said, *post coitum omne animal triste*. I began to cry, perhaps on account of the preceding stirring sensations. I burst into tears and he…he totally misunderstood my weeping. He said was I of the opinion a man could only express his love with a marriage certificate? Words failed me briefly. Then I called him an idiotic old macho who evidently felt the whole town wanted to marry him, I in any case was the last one to get myself on this waiting list, I still happened to be married–and during these words I was thinking with fierce satisfaction of the councilor–and I wasn't contemplating altering this state. He was to leave my bed at once and vanish forever. But he didn't go, instead he began to caress my hair and protested that he understood me, that he needed me, that he loved me, and into my stubbornly averted back he confessed his fear, his fear of losing me, of being left alone; he needed me but he also knew that I needed him too, he'd recognized that long ago, but he couldn't marry me, he wasn't able to financially, he had to take care of his three out-of-wedlock children and his handicapped sister, and finally he also had to support himself too. But his feeling of responsibility for me didn't permit him to define me only as lover because he thus felt petty and powerless. After this admission my emotional state changed completely. Suddenly, I felt very close to him; didn't he have the same anxieties I had? And the fact that he opened up to me, bared his weakness and love, led me—don't ask me how—to renew my passion for him. And suddenly I envisioned something like a future for us both if we supported each other in our need, and I decided to love him. I love him. What do you say now? I really believe that I love him. And now I also understand his reaction to my tears. Evidently up to now he has experienced weeping women only as marriage blackmailers, if you consider he has three children out of wedlock. I don't know if they're from one or two or three women. This morning when he was sneaking out of the house I was still asleep. I just called him and asked him, something I've never done before, if he'd like to sleep with me again today. "Actually we should just be sleeping," he laughed, "otherwise I'd wear myself out too much," but he would come to warm my cold feet. My schedule doesn't really allow this visit today, last week had been too turbulent, and I was beginning the new week completely exhausted. But still, I won't let him get away from me today. I'm looking forward to him, and on our next walk, I'll turn the tables and introduce him to my friends and Steyr society.

14.

Between the Calls

There's nothing new from the provincial Alpine foothills. What I'll now report is completely inconsequential, yet still typical for certain men in this land as well as for conforming, idiotic women of which I'm one. How I managed to talk myself into passion! I even thought I loved him! Yes, he came for a visit. During dinner he explained to me how he did not want his breakfast ham tomorrow wrapped in aluminum foil because it acquires a peculiar taste. Well then, I said, there won't be any ham for him for breakfast tomorrow. Slightly put out, he retired after dinner to my living room, lolled about in his jogging outfit on my leather chair and let me clear the table alone. Obviously, he felt very much like a guest in a restaurant, thought of me as his hostess for all occasions, and babbled on about Austria having been Hitler-Germany's first victim. While I was busy with the dishes in the kitchen, disposing of the rest of the food, I heard his sermon rushing past my ear, did not contradict because I was too tired. Finally, I had worked in the office until seven, raced home, quickly shopped in the grocery store, prepared a beef roast *à la crème*, cleaned the apartment until it sparkled, all the while having to rush to the bathroom a hundred times—bladder problem once again, or still—and at nine he made an appearance: the awaited one, Theodor; he is always very punctual. And after all my expectations: this sobering disenchantment. Instead of declarations of love, I now had to listen to his opinion of the theory of victimology. Suddenly, while I was still washing the dishes, the telephone rang. How I rejoiced when I heard Wolf's cheerful and eroticizing voice. He was filled with longing for me, and I was so frustrated by the boring topic of Austria as instigator or victim which the jurist, lounging on my couch, had forced on me as if we had no other concerns, that I left the room with my cell phone and Wolfram's voice in my ear, joked with my little Wolf in the bedroom and would have liked nothing better than up and away and into his arms. When I returned to my guest he asked me if I couldn't train my acquaintances better. To call at half past ten at night was an affront. Then he immediately returned to his topic, held under my nose his letter to the editor that had been printed in *The Format*, and in which he felt he had underpinned his thesis with irrefutable juridical subtlety. Nonetheless I still tried to contradict his doctrine of victimology, and I continued all the while doing the dishes. Then I went to brush my teeth, and at that point Wolfram called again. He had evidently noticed I wasn't quite as open as usual and wanted to know if I had visitors. A colleague was here, I said and really regretted not being able to talk to him freely; in this tiresome situation I would have preferred any vagrant crossing my path to the jurist. My guest was convinced the caller had been the veterinarian because otherwise I could have said that he, the jurist, was here with me. Then he began to reproach me for still not having broken off with the veterinarian and probably taking him back if he'd return, and saying that this "idiotic" councilor had no manners, otherwise he wouldn't be calling so late. I laughed until I cried, not so much because he assumed it was the councilor who had called but because he thought only he and the councilor had a place in my life–or in my heart. Not even remotely did it occur to him there could also be a third party. I was amused, yet I still felt exhausted. You have to realize that the weekend before, I washed seven loads of laundry, ironed sixteen shirts and twenty-six yards of office curtains, and cleaned and cooked for Mandi. In addition I still have my office worries as much as before, and so after brushing my teeth I didn't feel much like anything anymore. Theo, who had totally erred, attributed my lack of desire to a moral hangover associated with the councilor-veterinarian. He accused me of anachronistic moral concepts and grotesque subordination tendencies because the councilor merely had to call and I was as if transformed. It was, for me as well as for all women, a mere question of being married. I had heard enough, the joke went too far, and I ended the discussion. Now, I thought, now it's finally over and I felt relieved after I had thrown him out of the apartment. The next day a message arrived: *dear goldsweetie: may I come beddiebye tonight?* I did not reply. He also called and reproached me, saying he knew why I didn't reply; I had said "Wednesday" to the veterinarian on the phone, and now he was sure I would meet him today and then he added bitterly that would be in my best interest anyway since I had office worries after all. "Could very well be," I told Wolfram, "on Wednesday." The fact is he told me he was flying to Paris today and would return to St. Pölten tomorrow. I didn't feel like entertaining Theodor's paranoia. I was really irritated because the jurist evidently considers me incapable of surviving alone as a lawyer. He couldn't bear it if I were better than he was. And so he believed it was for economic reasons I wanted to renew my relationship with the veterinarian. I find it hurtful and dishonest of him because at the same time he's urging a union with me. From a professional consolidation he's expecting more profits, from a private alliance a decrease in his monthly expenditures and free domestic help. And on top of that his sex life is taken care of too. And all this he'd obtain without obligations, without a corresponding quid pro quo. Surely he can't be that obtuse to believe I could enter into such a proposition. I think nothing of the modern concept of a partnership for life. I want a lover and not a partner in life. Under these auspices the St. Pölten guy does seem more alluring. He's a dreamer, he's still urging me to come to St. Pölten, lately he's even made plans to go to Egypt and search for his father, and I'm to accompany him. But these are all illusions.

Next week will be a horror week. In my *causa prima* I have a three-day hearing before the provincial court of Wels, tomorrow an appointment with the regional newspaper and most likely next week with a news magazine; the data for the homepage have to be ready, the usual workload has to be carried out, Mandi is coming home again next weekend, and I still have to go through the mail and sign papers and then drive home at last. I won't have dinner before midnight. There is no room for a man in such a crazed existence. And because I've chatted with you on the phone for over an hour I still have to read tonight the document for tomorrow. It's like a penal colony around here.

One thing I've learned from my dealings with men: it's not worth the trouble to worry too much. I probably did have anachronistic ideas because I thought I had to decide as quickly as possible on one man merely because I was in bed with one and then the other. Wolfram just sent me a message. He's stuck in Paris. It was cold without me. At the airport he had bought a *flacon* of *Obsession* and sprayed some of it in the hotel room so that it would smell a little like me. If only he were here!

15.

Custody Petition

I haven't been to my office the past two days since I had the marathon hearing before the provincial court in Wels. During the trial I sat as a secondary plaintiff beside the district attorney and exerted all my charms to convince him to petition immediate custody. We're dealing with a real estate crook that also swindled my mother at one time, and I want him behind bars. During several of the lunches we had together I made strong efforts to convince the district attorney of my position, which seemed to have been successful because he promised to address the custody petition on Monday, and he also invited me to an evening stroll in Wels, his hometown. I don't know why I turned him down, maybe I suddenly wanted to appear serious and professional, in any case later on I had some regrets. Maybe I've simply had it with men and all my episodes with men; the feeling that I could if I wanted to made me feel cool and composed, and this composure stifled my desire. In decisive moments, I have come to realize, when one really would need someone, a shoulder to lean and weep on, there's no one there anyway. But also for laughing, for simple carefree happiness, there's seldom a man to be found. Besides, I would like to open a branch office in Kronstorf; that's on my mind at the moment, and that too I couldn't discuss with men. My expansionist striving makes them anxious, they immediately feel diminished, and they can't stand it. And it's this lack of generosity that really makes them appear small and ridiculous. I scorn them, all of them, particularly the jurist, who sent me lambskin house slippers in size 9. I happen to wear a size 6. Most likely he found them among his mother's or his aunt's belongings; several times already he's wanted to give me fur caps and even a mink coat weighing a ton from their estate. In his accompanying note he alluded to my bladder and my constantly cold feet since I no longer give him an opportunity to warm them. This package was waiting for me after I rushed home to get some rest instead of sauntering through Wels with the district attorney. Nothing in any case came of my rest because Wolfi's call reached me. He was on the autobahn and would be here in an hour. There went my good resolutions and my composure. He looked a little unkempt; I watched him with delight and anticipation, as he devoured vast amounts of my warmed-up stew. He brought me the opened bottle of *Obsession* and a CD with Bruckner's Fifth, talked me into displaying my modest skills on the piano, before he himself pounced on the keys and pounded out a few old hits. I played along, let him push me against the wall; he struck the keys furiously, and the neighbors called and threatened me with the police if this "racket" didn't stop at once. It was almost midnight, and we laughed uproariously about it; we had drunk quite a bit, but then we calmed down anyway–and I didn't sleep all night long. In this state I had to make my deposition at eight-thirty before the Wels Provincial Court; in the evening I was totally bushed. I had to hurry to get home because my apartment resembled a battlefield, and my Islamic guardian of public morals was going to arrive from Innsbruck; he mustn't discover the mess because otherwise I would be dismissed for good as a respectable role model. I also had no idea what to do with the insufferable house slippers and so I pushed them in their plastic bag under my bed. Surely the jurist, this ignoramus, must have noticed I can't stand house slippers, never wear any unless I'm being forced to wear them, and often enough I had railed against his leather slippers which he had taken to wearing in my apartment. I still remember a housewarming party at a colleague's. Forty invited guests were to admire his new, chic domicile. We all arrived elegantly attired, men with neckties and dark suits, the ladies in cocktail dress, decorated with jewels; yes, that's how conventional we still are. Naturally I was also wearing my pearls and a light bolero of silver mink over my low-cut, snug dress. But even before we could hand over our little presents, we, men as well as women, were compelled to slide into shapeless slippers which had been lined up in rank and file along the hallway. I was wearing my high-heeled Prada shoes for the first time, on which I prided myself quite a bit. Unfortunately I didn't dare to oppose the group pressure, and I'm still annoyed about it today. My sinfully expensive heels gleamed in vain as they were lined up with forty others along the corridor wall, and it pained my soul. In coarse felt slippers, in which you could only move forward with gliding motion, we accepted our welcome cocktail. Ill-humored, I gulped down my drink and was on the lookout for an ashtray. It turned out that smoking was not desired. These fur slippers from my ex-lover now reminded me of that frustrating evening. And yesterday when I had so much fun with Wolfram I also had to think of him; I saw him staring at the TV in his stuffy Bad Ischl apartment because that's precisely what he did, when suddenly at nine o'clock a message arrived: *You should turn on ZDF. There's a program on international real estate fraud. Could be important for your Wels trial.* As you can well imagine, a totally different program happened to be on for Wolfram and me, and I briefly thought he's merely driving me farther and farther away from him with such instructions. My secretary notified me that the district attorney from Wels had called and asked me to get back to him. That's pretty unusual behavior for the D.A.'s office; he might have misjudged me somewhat. I feel quite burned out; in spite of few new cases I'm still frightfully busy, but since I don't feel like working at all I'm talking to you on the phone for hours; I talk and talk, because if I stop I have the feeling all my problems dealing with men and the office and the world will cave in on me. I talk and talk, although as a child I was always forbidden to talk. "Don't always be the center of attention," my parents used to say to me as soon as I merely opened my mouth; they both agreed on that, and that's why today I still can't quite be very much in control. I'm not that much in demand, business is not that great. All I long for is a snowy-white sandy beach, with palm trees leaning over the deep blue sea, and I wish I could lie in their shade with a drink in one hand and a book in the other or look into the sky or out onto the sea. An affectionate man could also fit into this idyllic scene but I can't find one who'd undertake something like that with me. Such wishes don't bespeak presumption, do they? I find them modest, even touchingly modest. Every cleaning woman, every unskilled worker here can afford such a trip these days. If I had become a toilet cleaner, as my parents had always predicted, I'd definitely be lying under palm trees every year with a drink in my hand.

16.

Anticipation

I think I've always been afraid of Christmas. When I was a child my parents used to fight their marital battles precisely at Christmas time under the Christmas tree. I hadn't opened all my presents yet when my parents were already at loggerheads, as if the burning candles were inciting them to blaze up. I didn't understand what their fights were about but I felt guilty. Whenever my parents fought I thought it was my fault. One time, I had just unwrapped a doll, a doll with golden hair that I had longed for in the worst way, when the Christmas tree started to burn. My mother screeched. My father slapped the flames down with his hands. That was the only time I ever admired my father. But not for long, because the danger was barely over when I was scolded, since I was the one who had caused the mess with my magic candle. Later on, after I had married Walter, I was always waiting for a miracle at Christmas. It's the Christian religion that's responsible for making us believe miracles have to occur at Christmas. The Advent season already intensified one's anticipation, so for years I had high expectations of this holiday, something that the holiday never could live up to. I myself didn't know what I wanted. Maybe some kind of a compensation for my bungled childhood, for which Walter was to compensate me. That never worked. And now, now I'm more afraid than ever of Christmas because I'll be alone with Mandi and I imagine, against my better judgment, that everywhere else behind those brightly lit windows are happy families celebrating. I was wondering how much longer it would be before I'm completely alone, Mandi would leave me at some point; at first I'd be all alone and then no longer existing at all. A longing for love arose in me then, a longing for the pleasures of life, I still had so much to catch up on. The question is only whether this passionate life I desired is truly more intense, or simply sapping my strength. I can't bear getting old, least of all with equanimity and composure. Suddenly one grows old. I saw that happening with my mother; until sixty she looked almost youthful, three years later she was an old woman. One day I'll also wake up an old woman, and not even the jurist will call me and want me. Besides, his business is not going well, and the child support he's paying for his brats is leaving him destitute. I almost felt pity for him. I shouldn't have gotten involved with him because in this weakened condition I also don't feel like abusing him, and so I put up with him, yet his lack of success makes him less and less attractive to me. Business failures simply don't exude sex appeal. Still, I visited him on the 23rd of December. I took him a Pelican fountain pen bought at the last moment, and he presented me with a cell phone with the instruction to leave this gadget at home at all times so that he could always reach me there. Often I didn't pick up when the caller ID displayed his name; on the following day I could pretend I had forgotten it at the office. I no longer have this excuse. He also surprised me with an outrageously expensive perfume by Balmain and explained that it smelled *superb*. I hate it when someone gives me a new perfume. I use Calvin Klein's *Obsession* and nothing else. Then he also bought me videos, musicals, which I never could stand. And it was only for me that he had decorated a Christmas tree, although I also can't stand those. After half a bottle of whisky I didn't feel like getting into the car and making the long drive back to Steyr, so I spent the night with him. Actually I have lots of friends, colleagues, male and female, but on super-sacred holidays no one is available, which is a sign that I've done something wrong. A former female client of mine whose business was a virtual failure and who, with my legal assistance, got back on her feet again and is now thriving exceptionally, invited me for New Year's Eve after my mother had died and I was quite depressed. Today she repeated her invitation but I declined because I'm embarrassed that I'm still so alone and so needy. Should I have accepted? She would have been happy. Was I arrogant? Of course I had counted on Wolfram, but once again he failed to make an appearance; his business interests took precedence. I desperately longed for this man and was terribly disappointed. Perhaps, he announced, he'd come next week, but I said that I would be busy then, which wasn't true at all, but I wanted to keep him up in the air. But most likely it's not he, but rather myself, who's dangling in the net I've cast for him. And because I was alone, I invited Theodor for dinner. Mandi was still at home. Pretty soon we started complaining about our work. Then he began again to talk about consolidating our two offices, going so far as to claim it was mainly for my benefit. It was an awfully uncomfortable evening. Mandi grinned in tormented fashion the entire time. I felt sorry for him. The jurist wouldn't leave for the longest time and I didn't know how to get rid of him without provoking a scene in front of Mandi. But on the next day another message arrived: *is my elfisweetie coming tomorrow?* I did not come. I spent New Year's Eve all alone. Sat at the piano and jingled a few tunes, hoping ridiculously to be able to impress Wolfram next time with my playing. Mandi stopped by briefly, but left shortly afterwards to celebrate with friends. Finally I did become somewhat melancholy, all alone. I recapitulated and analyzed and had to determine that all the things concerning me personally were not controlled by me but rather I let myself be controlled. An old habit from a bad marriage: I abdicated all responsibility. And now I know what matters—a true partner. A partner who does not vanish when he's had enough but endures and supports and tolerates in good as well as in bad days, as the saying goes. Then I remembered that I had stopped menstruating months ago, and I thought: *Now you're old, now you'll start to dry up, and your hair will thin out and a little beard will grow on your upper lip.* Then I caught sight of my stomach, which had begun to stick out, and I had also gained weight. I stood in front of the mirror in my tight Wolford skirt, and I felt sick, in fact lately I felt sick quite often. Then the crazy fear came over me that I could be pregnant. I wouldn't even know who the father was. I was beside myself and called my gynecologist the next day and he only underlined my uncertainty by saying nothing could be ruled out. Do you consider pregnancy at my age possible? Actually there's nothing I'd wish for more than another baby. I wish I could report to you tomorrow…yes, what is it that I want?

17.

Ear Noises

Of course I'm not pregnant, it would have been a medical miracle. There's no child growing in my belly, just fat. It's not the belly of a pregnant woman, just the potbelly of an aging one. Haven't you noticed how women when they age, even if they are slender, yes, even skinny, always get a paunch? They grow a kind of pointed belly that they carry like a ship's prow in front of them; while the bosom shrinks, old women's bellies mature, while their chest cavity becomes hollow, their back becomes bent, and a hump thrives there. How much destructive energy the Creator must possess to endow his creatures with such perfidious physical dissolution. During my period of anxiety or anticipation—in any case during the time of uncertainty, which my gynecologist even managed to stoke with his "nothing could be ruled out"—it became clear to me what I was doing to myself. Don't you think I'm a self-supplier in the inflicting of pain? I let everything happen, and I let myself in for everything. Neither of the two men, no man, deserves that. Neither would support me if things got serious, I couldn't have informed either of the potential fathers. I mustn't continue like this. I have seriously resolved, yes, made a serious promise to myself that I will not permit anyone to hurt me anymore and I will break off contacts that do me no good. To be precise, however, I'd have to break off contact with myself because often enough I've hurt myself. But I have only one ego. The ego knows no dualism, and so I must learn to deal better with myself. I wrote all this to St. Pölten—that I wouldn't ever become involved with him again because he always succeeded in hurting me terribly. That's not easy for me because I like men. After years of abstinence I felt sufficiently strong to love again—no, to love for the first time. I love this man, this Wolf, this wild animal, and for this very reason I have to banish him from my life and eradicate my emotions. I would have done anything for this man. I also would have ruined myself financially for him. Often I sat for hours by the phone and longed for his call, will he call, should I call him? Whenever I lost my nerve and was the first to call I was once again the weaker one. If he called I briefly felt relief. I could have soared. But already a few hours later I was waiting for the next call. I worked without concentration, lacked discipline. I spent twelve hours or more in the office although I could have taken care of the pertinent files and dossiers in less time. He is the stronger one. I wanted to lean on this man, a macho, even if he does pretend to be a real softie. Don't ever, please, talk me into this monster. It's difficult enough for me not to jump into the car and drive to St. Pölten.

The District Attorney from Wels also got in touch with me again; I went out to dinner with him, then we said goodbye, he intended to call again. Let him! I sold Mother's piano; with the proceeds I'll buy myself drums. I've already found a teacher who could show me how to play. Of course I don't know if I'll enjoy beating the drums in the long run but now I need them to work off my aggressions. To bang the drums, to learn how to strike, that's what's called for. And every time my fingers itch and I want to dial his number I'll start to hit the drums and beat them like mad. Go ahead and laugh at me! The other day I could have used the instrument, I would have gone to town on the drums. A middle-aged man came into my office and inquired: "Is no one here?" I said, "Yes, of course, I'm here as you can see." "Yes, I can see, but where is Dr. Schweiger?" "Dr. Schweiger, that's me." When he realized there was no male attorney, merely a woman, he fled. I wonder how many men have run away when they heard they're dealing with a female attorney! Recently a female colleague and I visited a nightclub at 10 o'clock in Steyr's historic district. Two men, at first glance thoroughly likeable and good-looking, helped us out of our coats and immediately started to flirt with us. They asked us about our jobs. Since we evidently still are used to letting ourselves be questioned, we replied, like good girls, we were attorneys. Then they felt as if we had taken them for a ride and shortly afterwards they took off. Tell me, what job should I acquire for a flirtation. Kindergarten teacher? Elementary schoolteacher? Hairdresser? Then they could still show off and pretend to be real devil-dogs. But with a female attorney they don't dare to open their mouths, afraid something might slip out that could be used against them. I need a drum, tympani, sticks and cymbals; with these I will deaden my longing for this impossible sex, I will execute a kind of voodoo-magic, fall into a trance. Today I had to toil all day and find out whether a universal succession from an inheritance agreement has a three-year or thirty-year statute of limitation. My former boss in Amstetten always used to say, "Colleague, be brave with regard to a loophole. Sometimes you have to take risks, otherwise you spend days hovering over every document, and you can't do that for economic considerations." My job is the shittiest. I envy every toilet cleaner because she can sleep at least; after she's locked up her little outhouses and comes home she goes to bed and has come to terms with herself, but I will be plagued by a thousand doubts because of this document. My colleagues Watzlawik and Krobath also couldn't help me out. I had to keep my fingers crossed that the suit wouldn't be rejected. I wasted the whole day on it. I took my finished product to the post office and trembled. Tomorrow I have two deadlines. Another one of my clients is going bankrupt. He's the region's biggest building contractor and this will lead not only to the loss of many jobs and weaken my own income but also inflict damage on the economic strength of the area.

I've been taken in by the jurist once again, but definitely for the last time. He asked to have a talk with me and the result is that I now have to run around wearing a scarf. I hate scarves. It's been at least a week now that I've been running around with the jurist's mark under the scarf. Actually I should make him give me one of these extravagantly expensive, exquisite pashminas as compensation but then I'd have to feel obligated again. I must grant him one thing, this man is not stupid, but let me qualify this right away. To twist a fool around your little finger doesn't require great intelligence. He arranged it cleverly. First we met in a café to have our arranged talk, then he suddenly got hungry and off we went to Raddampfer, a top restaurant. He knows I'm totally starved in the evenings and will consume everything. There he made me drunk, turned on the sympathy machine and flattered me with compliments;

for once he did not lecture on Greco-Turkish history, he also did not discuss the origin of papal humility rituals, nor did he call me "Kittiesweetie" or "Elfilocks" and I, smashed as I was, went to bed with him. Even before I discovered this hideous blue-red spot on an exposed area on my neck in the bathroom mirror I knew there is no happy end with him. Train him? No, one can't train a man. Nor do I want to. In this regard I already failed with my dog, which by the way I miss again. My beautiful Afghan virtually never obeyed me; I was barely able to teach her to "shake hands," and that worked only if she smelled some ham. If I can't even succeed with a dog, how can I do it with a man who, you'll have to admit, has a more complex structure? I'm not interested in spending my lonely hours with merely anyone. I'm expecting a lot from a partner. There's so much lacking for me to cope well with my life. It all started in my childhood, with the make-up of my family. The unresolved dissonances in the relationship between the parents' character and convictions continue to resound in the nature of the child and create its inner story of suffering, says Nietzsche. Of course ultimately I stood my ground quite well in this tension-filled arena, I got my revenge as far as my father is concerned. But more important than my revenge would have been his love. Thank you for always listening to me. Talking, teens, forced to work after school and contribute to their families. That didn't matter much either, though. Status was irrelevant, money was fake, and the future was preordained.

I could feel the parasites throbbing inside my body, eagerly trying to horrify me, but it just wasn't working. As I dunked a young black girl's head into the deep fryer, I was all pins and needles. Even as I continued to hold her head under the hot bubbling oil and felt her skin blistering against my hand, there was zero emotional reaction.

When the parasites had me take hold of the knife on the cutting board and butcher the remaining staff, I wasn't even trying to fight them anymore. I was just going along with it, going through the motions. Even when I lopped a young man's prick from his pubic region and absent-mindedly sucked on it in front of the terrified customers, it felt so mundane.

I must have stabbed them a thousand times. The sum of the mayhem was beyond my calculation. When they were all dead, I lined up the entire grill with teenage cock and titties. But it all just looked like hotdogs and hamburgers to me.

***

On the third round I recalled that they tried to get to you. To fuck with your head. To make it personal and intimately catastrophic. The first two simulations seemed so generic now that I knew what I knew. They were undoubtedly the product of poor primal programming by the Thorns. But the last one, well, that one was a real mother fucker.

Janie sat at one end of a table and I sat at the other. There was a full meal between us and we were flanked by the dead rotting corpses of her children. Bell and Alicia both had blackened skin that was in the advanced stages of decomposition. Their little slimy shells had become rife with maggots and worms. The flesh pulsated and squirmed, finding a foul life of its own.

Janie couldn't quite grasp the concept that they were

dead. She was acting much different than I'd ever seen before. She rose to her feet and approached baby Bell asking questions that she knew couldn't be answered.

"Do you want to take a bite for momma? No? Not even a little one?" she asked, pressing a spoon filled with mashed potatoes against her lips.

An ebony fluid expelled from her tiny mouth and nasal cavity. The stew of spit and decomposition spurted out onto the spoon discoloring the wad of mashed potatoes.

"You are going to eat little girl, rest assured. If you want to grow up to be big and strong, you have to," Janie said.

She cocked the spoon all the way back and then drove it forward into Bell's decaying grimace. Some of the tissue was soft enough that it caved in and separated. Even more bugs were housed inside the child's ghastly interior. Earwigs, millipedes, and cockroaches galore left the child's mutilated maw, spilling all over her booster seat.

"You're letting out much more than you're taking in, now I wonder why that is?" When Janie finished speaking, she turned toward me. I noticed her teeth were now black and wet and her face suddenly had patches of discoloration swelling all over her skin.

"NO! Your mouth doesn't work anymore!" she cried.

Her demeanor disturbed me. The look on her face wasn't how I wanted to remember her. She was rife with madness and savagery.

"Now I'll never be able to hear your voice! I'll never be able to talk to you! You're just a whining sack of misery! A curse!" She lifted the plate of food off the table and set it crashing against the infant corpse.

As the hole above the child's head opened up further, her admittedly fictitious words cut me deep. I hadn't thought of that aspect. I'd killed Janie's daughters before they could even utter a word.

Would she have wanted to talk to them someday?! Would she have preferred they died after gaining the ability to speak?! I wondered.

The more I thought about it, the more I started to

consider the possibility that she might actually be upset when she saw me. As I watched the demonic rendition of Janie pull handfuls of bugs out from Bell and eat them, I felt worry worming its way through me.

Could this be a dealbreaker?

Janie pulled up a silver plate cover and revealed the same teethy, hairy, slimy parasites that had once again left my exit wet. The snide little bastards arranged the teeth to generate the ultimate fractured smile. As if to say, 'Didn't think of that one, now did you?'

The sad part was that they were fucking right. The little abominations had somehow found a way to get inside my head yet again.

There was more screaming, more violence, and more chaos from Janie's deranged doppelgänger, but the real damage was already done. It was psychological. As she tore her children limb from limb, I sat numb.

Awaiting the same pink goop to leech onto me and advance me forward.

Awaiting a potential meeting with the toddlers I'd just murdered.

Before I was forced to witness this hellish theater, I had it all figured out. But now the white knight that was set to return and save the day had blood on his hands. Suddenly, the celebrational return was in doubt. And my macabre, backwards heroism would soon be up for judgement.

JUDGEMENT DAY

When the lights finally came back on, I was in the flesh tunnel again like before. And to Fink's credit, just as he'd explained, baby Bell and little Alicia were each crying and crawling just a few yards away from me. Just like anyone else in the realm, no tears dribbled down their faces, but the pain that laid ahead of us would be felt.

So far, the process itself had been almost exactly the same aside from the murder simulations. While the themes weren't identical, the format was; there were still three. Which led me to believe that if I ventured down the hall with the children, it would only be a short time before all of us encountered the Thorns and their demonic tortures again. We were awaiting a vile juicing of our darkest experiences by their prickly hands. But did we have to move forward?

The Thorns! That's it!

I didn't know if it would work, but it was certainly worth a shot. I tried to push through my exhaustion and pulled the young ones into my arms, attempting to calm their fears. In all likelihood I was probably just adding to their dread, being that I was the last face they'd seen before their descent. I didn't want them to relive that, to think of me that way every time they looked at me.

I closed my eyes with them snuggled against my chest and focused. I potentially had one ace up my sleeve, an inside man. But I didn't know if Belthorn had access to the reentry space where we were currently confined to.

Belthorn? Belthorn? Can you hear me? I know it's been some time, but it's Andy. I've returned… I need to ask another favor of you. Can you bring us back to eternity? Can you spare us further torment?

I'd witnessed his psychic abilities and link to the world of the living. His kindness was the only hope I had.

Please, Belthorn, bring us salvation! We need to find Janie!

As the thought screeched around in my brain, I heard the wall beside me start to rumble. The gory claustrophobia parted, and suddenly, I heard a voice speak to me through the cries of the young.

"You must go now! Quickly! I cannot keep it open for long!" Belthorn's tone echoed.

I picked up the girls and ran forward, like the devil himself was chasing after me. In a way he was. I could see a crimson light at the end of the darkness but I could feel the catacomb tube closing in behind me. The meat nipped at my heels as I tried to accelerate. I was almost there.

With the girls close to my heart, I dove out of the portal as it closed up behind me. I looked back with Bell in one arm and Alicia in the other, and took in the vast plane of nothingness. When I twisted in the opposite direction, I recognized the structure before me: Fink's tooth castle.

"Good luck, my friend, and may you find the happiness that I know you deserve," Belthorn's voice whispered before trailing off into the distance.

"Thank you," I replied.

I didn't know what else to say. I had no idea how things might've turned out without his help and knowledge. He was a good dude. I hoped it wouldn't be the last time our paths crossed.

The children had stopped crying, as if Belthorn's calming voice quelled their worries. I worked my way to my feet and once again approached the yellow incisor that I'd seen Fink twist to the left to open the front door.

I set the girls down for a moment and followed his exact actions, just as I'd remembered them. As I turned the tainted tooth, the familiar area of meat made way for us. Once I took hold of the girls and stepped inside, I was greeted by the lord of meat mountain himself.

"That was fast… I think. Everything kind of feels really fast or really slow depending on how you look at it. I guess you were in a coma? I see you've brought some friends with you. Come, Janie's upstairs," he explained, turning toward the elevator of warm cells beside him.

"Wait! Please," I begged.

He turned back toward me a bit puzzled, "What is it?"

"You knew I was coming. Does Janie know?" I asked.

"Belthorn told me. It doesn't happen often, but I find it incredibly creepy when his voice just appears in my head. It's an invasion of privacy! But, it's for a good cause, I suppose… As far as Janie goes, since you left, she hasn't moved a muscle. She's essentially gone mute; I can't get a word out of her. Seems like she's just waiting. What she's waiting for, only she knows," Fink explained.

"Alright," I mumbled, not sure what else he could say that was going to make this easier.

I took comfort in knowing that Janie didn't see me actually murder them, but seeing us together, she'll know. What will her reaction be? Will she hate me for doing what I thought she wanted? For robbing her of the option to ever have a conversation with her spawns? Did I know her well enough to properly predict her preference?

telling stories, has become my analgesic. As long as I'm speaking into your open ear my suffering is silent. I talk and talk until I don't feel any more pain. With my sentences I squeeze everything out of me, empty myself out. Sometimes I feel like a Scheherazade who keeps herself alive by talking. In discussion even terrible events take on energizing components, do you understand that? Shared passion is doubled; shared suffering is halved. I first had to become conscious of this banality; instinctively I reached for the telephone when I couldn't bear it any longer and dialed your number. And when you lent me your ear I knew I would survive. Does this sound too pathetic?

I love men but will not let any come close to me ever again, I swear to you. The closer they came to me the more disappointing they were and the more they hurt me and misused me for their purposes. The St. Pölten fellow wanted to use me as a car salesman for his dead-end Mazda firm, and the jurist saw me as a cost cutter for his office. From now on I will put men to my use. The veterinarian, who had committed himself months ago to paying the repair bill for Mandi's DVD-system, still hasn't paid it. Besides, he is expecting me to assume the extra expenses for Mandi because the boy is not studying enough. It's true, unfortunately, that he failed his exam in vegetation studies again. He's been studying forestry for nine semesters already and hasn't completed even his first stage of studies. Under these circumstances it's not easy to coax money out of the father for the son. I'm beginning to hate this man and told him he's the biggest asshole I know and threatened not to speak another word with him if he doesn't fulfill his paternal duties. I lost all self-control and that did me a world of good. And a little later on, I was in super form, the District Attorney called. I had actually forgotten his first name. Still, I was suddenly tempted to channel the conversation into other directions. I followed him to his museum, he founded a museum for fire department and spraying techniques, and then I abducted him to Florence, to the Accademia, where he's never been, and began to rave about Michelangelo's *David*, this muscular adolescent body. Afterward, I asked him if he knew of a female sculpture that he finds desirable, so desirable that he could fall in love with it. He couldn't come up with anything, so I suggested Lehmbruck's *Kneeling Woman* or Maillol's *Flora*, he wasn't familiar with them, but finally Claudia Schiffer occurred to him; he liked her pretty well. You won't believe it, don't ask me how, but I was able to guide him from Claudia Schiffer to me, to my body. And after I had conjured up what I intended to conjure up I suddenly broke off the conversation in disgust.

Mandi called me from Innsbruck. He sounded pretty subdued. He wants to give up his forestry studies. He claimed he never really had taken an interest in the forest. His true inclination (you won't believe what's coming next), his true inclination is the law. He's sensed this predilection for quite some time, however he'd tried to suppress it. He's coming back to me, and wants to study law in Linz! In five years he would be able to finish his studies, I'll support him as I did during his university entrance exams. Then I'll offer him a position as an assistant in my office and finally a partnership: Dr. Elfriede Schweiger and Son. With my son as a partner I could move my office to Linz, directly into the main square. The veterinarian, as was to be expected, raged and refused any further financial aid for Mandi. His son had no legal claim to support for a second course of studies. Whereupon I told him, yes, I was well aware of the fact since my father too didn't pay anything for me and instead wasted it on his floozie. But I would not abandon my son, I told him proudly. Just a moment… I see an e-mail from Wolf in my Inbox. Can you believe it, he wants to give up his car business and move with his computer into my place in Steyr. He's now specializing in the creation of *websites*. He's dying to practice his new profession in my apartment. He must have lost his mind. What is he thinking, that's impossible. I don't even know him. At the same time a text message from the jurist. He's pleading: *let me make it all up to you.* And again another e-mail from St. Pölten… Just a second, the doorbell is ringing. Mandi? No, it's the councilor. But he can stay outside.

G. Meyer Books specializes in autobiographical and fictional narratives that intersect with social, historical, and political issues, as well as books on contemporary social issues that vary from the norm and encourage questioning and debate. Inquiries regarding submissions may be sent to the G. Meyer Books website at http://www.gmeyerbooks.com.

 G. MEYERBOOKS

As I stepped into the meat box cradling the now quiet children, I knew, one way or another, I was about to find out. When the elevator finally came to a halt, I was filled with panic inside. I wished that I could just flash forward to the reveal and get it over with.

Janie was laid out on the moist flesh couch, resting her head uncomfortably upon an abnormally shaped tooth. She was facing toward the back support of the couch as if she didn't want to be bothered, staring blankly at the ruby exterior.

Fink stood quietly behind me, studying my anxiety with curiosity. I didn't know what to say. I thought about it for a moment, but no explanation arrived. I decided I would just remind her how I felt.

"Janie, I love yo—"

As the words left my lips a mind-shattering ring ripped through the airwaves. It sounded like a bell was being rung by a giant. The volume was so incredible that it felt like it was inside my fucking skull.

Janie turned around from her position and so did I. I looked back at Fink and asked, "What the fuck is that?"

His normally minuscule eyes were massive and wide and filled with something I'd never seen in them before: fear. His hearty lips opened as the three of us began to levitate.

"The lottery!" he yelled. "Hold onto each other, try to stay together!"

Janie's face was a melting pot of emotion. I saw pain, love, excitement, fear, horror, agony, and happiness all pulling her in different directions.

She had heard Fink's directions and hooked onto my bicep. Janie stroked baby Bell's face once she got close enough. She looked back up at me like she wanted to say something, but before she could, the ringing struck again.

As Fink wrapped his chubby digits around my ankle, my hearing was mashed by the deafening resounding waves. They blocked out my natural sense. I felt frozen in time, as we all drifted through the gaping holes in the side of Fink's mountain and up to a larger platform in the sky.

Not only had we ascended, but all the others, as far as the eye could see, were floating upward along with us. The platform was different than anything I'd seen in eternity to that point. It was ghostly, comprised of white, streaky, and almost spectral material. The outlandish scene was the stuff of big-budget movies.

As we made it over the space, high enough to be placed, I started to understand just how colossal it was. The people were in such abundance that they looked like bugs. A never-ending army of ants, making me feel more insignificant than I'd ever considered.

In the center of the nexus was an orb or light that was by far the biggest structure I'd ever seen. An electric lime barrier encapsulated it. I watched it jump around violently as whatever force had been controlling us, finally set us down amid a cluster of our fellow species.

Upon landing my arms went limp and both Bell and Alicia landed at my sides. The five of us stood beside each other, Janie holding Bell in one arm and Alicia's hand with the other. We looked up at the otherworldly display, all equally awestruck. The harsh ringing continued to dominate my hearing.

I assumed it was the same for everyone else. My body was rigid, all but my facial features. I moved my mouth, trying to power through whatever was controlling me. I tried to ask Janie if she was alright, but I couldn't hear my words through the noise, and assumed she couldn't either.

A deep trumpet suddenly added to the equation, the dark sinister notes sounding like something you might hear on Earth to signify that the world was ending. The noise was absolutely terrifying.

Then, suddenly, everything stopped. The gargantuan orb began to glow with brilliance and pulsate. I could feel my mouth getting hot. I could feel the normally gamey and resilient muscle that comprised my tongue quivering wildly. A ghastly putrid porridge started to leak out of my jaws.

Suddenly, I realized that I no longer had a tongue, and I felt the scorching liquified remnants sizzling on my sternum as they drizzled from my oral crack.

The numbers! I thought. *The lottery…*

I didn't know what came next, but I had figured out what was happening. As I began to elevate back into the sky and toward the electrical globe above, I could see that I wasn't the only one. Amid the billions that comprised the sea of humanity on the poltergeist platform, a few thousand others ascended with me.

In the grand scheme of things, those ascending were just a tiny fraction of the crowd we were leaving behind. I had been chosen, but chosen for what exactly? I recalled Fink's clue about the lottery, a conversation that we'd never really had the chance to finish: "What do you get if you win?" I asked. "It's not like that," Fink replied, "nobody *wins* this lottery."

As my body twirled and contorted in the strange stratosphere, I was close enough to the ground still to zero in on Janie's face. She was moving her mouth and I could see there was a deep agony suctioned to her face, like her heart was being ripped out.

I couldn't be sure that she said 'I love you,' I wasn't a lipreader, but it sure looked that way. I tried to respond, wanting more than anything just to tell her the same. Had I still been equipped to, I would have sold my soul to transmit the message. It was probably the most important thing I ever had to say.

My eyes didn't want to leave her beautiful face. I had no clue if it was the last time I'd be able to see it. But there was something inside me both telling me to look behind her and not to. A war of conscience doing battle on the spot. My nagging curiosity got the better of me, and sometimes I wish it hadn't.

Behind Janie, Fink, Bell, and Alicia, stood none other than the deranged psychopath Phillip Marks. Amid the chaos and panic of our initial decent, I wasn't paying too much attention to the details. In part it was because I simply couldn't. My figure was frozen as well as my mind. I floated helplessly, in awe of the entire activity that was transpiring.

In that moment, his would have been just another disturbed face in the crowd of heathens. But now that I was leaving, the dastardly distinction was glaring. His expression conveyed that he was incredibly excited to see Janie alone, separated from me. The disturbed grin stretching ear to ear was the last thing I saw before I entered the light. As my body shook violently and I entered the voltage, I imagined that, for Phillip, it was a dream come true.

THE RELIGION OF REPETITION

I stayed in the pale blinding light for some time. I was still able to stay conscious, but I couldn't really grasp what was happening to me. My vision was blurred by the angelic ambiance and my body was immobilized. All I had during that time were my thoughts.

Where am I going?
What didn't Fink explain to me?
Will I ever see Janie and the girls again?

I could only imagine the answers. And nothing I seemed to imagine felt too promising. Unless this was somehow a minor detour from eternity, I'd never have a chance to ask or hunt down an answer. Sadly, the grandiose nature and sheer spectacle that 'winning' the lottery was, didn't afford me much confidence that that would be the case. The only thing that I kept coming back to was that it felt typical.

Typical of my life and times. This just seemed to be how things were for me. My existence was a tease. A sickening fifteen-minutes-of-fame kind of joke.

I felt detached and far away from anything or anyone I knew. I felt man's greatest fear; the unknown, taunting me and pulling at my emotions. The whole experience was a phantasmal roller coaster. One I found myself wondering if I'd ever get off of.

In my head I was still grateful that I'd gotten to spend the time I did with Janie. As horrific as much of it was, the highs filled me with more elation than I knew I was capable of experiencing. But then there was the other part…

On the flip side of the coin, there was the void. The hole in my soul that left me scarred. The idea that I might never see Janie again. The idea that Phillip Marks was eyeing her upon my exit and I wouldn't be there to protect her.

What would he do to her and the children?

The thought left me with a sensation of nausea with no way to act upon it. Another question came to me. I had been given so much information, the mother lode of knowledge, yet still, so much was missing.

It wasn't my own personal question. It was a repackaging of one that was often present in the popular culture that no longer seemed relevant to me. The society that I was a slave to a lifetime ago.

I couldn't remember who actually said it, I was never good with recalling that kind of detail. It was something along the lines of 'Is it better to have loved and lost than to never have loved at all?' I used to scoff at people that asked themselves that. I thought it was a privilege to even be in that position and attained the experience. But now that I was asking it myself, I wasn't so sure. For better or worse, I finally understood the notion.

As I jetted through the ivory oblivion, I'd lost all sense of time. The porcelain punishment that surrounded me was directionless. I could feel the energy around me causing my body to quake cruelly, until eventually I couldn't feel it at all.

***

When the flamingo flesh returned it was out of nowhere. The pearly ethereal tones felt like they'd been wiped away with one final brushstroke, and suddenly, I was aimless.

But this moist, rouge shade that surrounded me wasn't quite the same as the one that eternity was comprised of. I suddenly felt various amounts of pressure nudging me slightly in different directions. The nudges would come at random times.

I also noticed that I was immersed in some kind of translucent hot fluid. I could see, but my neck didn't feel strong enough to move, so I only saw what was in front of my eyes. I became a bit claustrophobic. I wasn't controlling it, but at times my leg would have an involuntary kicking reaction.

When the toes jumped forward, I could only catch a glimpse of them momentarily. My foot looked raw, like it had been deteriorated. Then suddenly, a thought struck me: what if it hadn't deteriorated at all? What if it was growing? I had no idea what to think of it. Even if I did settle on a feeling, there wasn't much I could do with it. As each unsettling moment drew on, I was feeling less and less like myself.

***

I was all smiles until I returned.

I'd somehow finally found my purpose in an irrational existence. I had an acceptable life after desperately clawing my way through each agonizing phase of my lonesome course. Through my pitiful childhood, and then into my forlorn, unfulfilling twenties. To when I was murdered and the curtain was pulled back. To the brief climax where I fell in love with the woman I was meant to be with.

Then finally, I moved on to my downward spiral. When I watched the tiniest flash of victory get ripped away from me. I could only equate it to the kissing game I'd heard other kids speak about playing as a child. I'd had my seven minutes in heaven, and apparently that was all I was going to get.

At times, I thought that it was just given to me so I could experience the heartache of it being taken away. Did the Thorns have a tracking system that carried over into eternity? If so, this would've been exactly the type of trauma that tickled them.

When I was born again, I wondered how I still had my memories from before. Trapped in the fragile frame of a newborn baby was terrifying. Knowing what I knew, I was a helpless and submissive seed. I had no other choice than to just linger.

I was a quiet baby girl, depressed really. I didn't cry or pine for attention. I just wanted to be left alone. Most parents would say that's a good baby. But now I wondered if all the babies that behaved were just the recycling of aged personalities from the spirits of dead men and women. I wondered if I would always have the memories, or if one day they might just evaporate like dewdrops on the grass on a hot summer day.

I had some point of reference. I recalled a podcast that I had listened to during my last life that tackled the topic of children who remember past lives. The stories were bizarre and largely inexplicable.

I hadn't done much research on it but remembered some of the highlights. Whether a few thirty-something-year-olds drinking beers, discussing paranormal events, cryptids, the unexplained, and conspiracies, could be taken at their word was questionable, but the more I thought about it the more sense it made.

They dove into a few cases, one that had particularly garnered my interest. It was about a boy in Ireland who had recited nearly seventy facts about his past life.

The boy was able to recall details as specific as the streets which he'd previously lived on, the names of his wife's sisters, and even occupational duties. All of which somehow turned out to be true.

Pulitzer Prize-winning author and Harvard professor John E. Mack had even investigated the strange event. A man that was highly respected in the educational and psychiatric community was unable to find any cracks in the case. His conclusion was that the boy was telling the truth.

Mack went on to do further studies on the topic and, eventually, he deduced that if the reincarnation was real, the only plausible explanation for everyone not remembering their past lives, was that, over time, we all just eventually forget. Even the subjects that he'd studied for years, lost their memories of their past lives between six and eight-years-old.

In addition, he also theorized that everyone might actually remember their past lives for some span of time. And the reason that there weren't more reports on the subject could be that many of them simply lost the information before they were old enough to convey it to anyone that would take it seriously. There was also no telling how many cases hadn't been brought to light as a result of religious reasons, or just people telling their children to stop mentioning it, figuring they were telling childish fabrications to gain more attention.

If that was the case there was no telling how long my mind would retain the memories of Janie and I. In my current body, how could I ever hope to see her again? Furthermore, would she even accept me now? I wouldn't even be able to talk to her.

I had a lot to sort out, and if there was any credence to the timeframe that Mack had placed on the children who remember past lives, I had little time to do it. It was a frightening thought, but I had no idea how to, or if I even wanted to, move on.

THE DEFINITION OF INSANITY

I had kept an eye on the calendar whenever Mom brought me into the kitchen. I took notice of how many months had passed whenever I had an opportunity to. The best I could figure it, about three years had gone by.

I was able to say simple words but not convey any kind of message. I was able to walk pretty decent, which gave me a chance. I could feel little pieces of my memory fading with each day that passed. I didn't know how much longer I had.

Most importantly, I could ascertain that I was still looking for the first opportunity to kill myself.

I didn't want to repeat the entire pointless cycle again. I couldn't see myself going through the motions for another lifetime. When I considered it, the entire concept felt so exhausting. I needed to act before I forgot that my sole purpose was just to be a form of amusement for the Thorns.

I could remember little else. I knew I wanted to die, but each day I struggled to recall exactly why. It was Jamie, wasn't it? Or was it Janie? There were other people where I was trying to go, I think. Why did I need to see her? Was she my momma from before? She felt like a warm and fuzzy momma. Not like the one I have right now. She didn't seem too nice. She seemed like a real bad lady actually. Maybe that's why Poppa left?

Just like today, every single day she would bring me into this room. But she will never play with me! She just drinks and drinks and drinks from her own bottle! And hers is much bigger and heavier than mine.

When I drink from my bottle, I get happy and I want to play. But my momma just falls asleep. But it's good that she falls asleep, because then I can maybe get past the gate.

At the top of the stairs there's a big gate that's supposed to keep me safe. Momma said never to go down the stairs alone, but why did I want to? Oh, yeah! I wanna fall down the stairs and die! But why? I don't know, but I want to. Momma's asleep again, so now's my chance!

I had seen how she got it to work before. I tugged at the gate and pulled it as hard as I could. It took me a few tries but it was open now! I put my feet on the very top step and looked down the big stairs.

They looked so crazy!

Why did I open the gate again? I looked at the step below and saw my Mr. Frog stuffed animal. That's right! I wanted my froggy to play with me since Momma wouldn't. That's why I opened the gate! Right?

Why else would I!? HAHA! I can't wait to play with him now! I thought, putting the gate right where it was before.

I didn't want to make Momma mad at me when she woke up. Maybe if she thought I was good she would play with me and Mr. Frog!

I looked over to the television on the other side of the room. There were a bunch of other kids sitting together. They looked like they were having so much fun!

I liked watching the TV with Mr. Frog! It always kept my brain busy while Momma was lazy sleeping. It made me happy to see the boys and girls just like me play with each other and sing and dance. They were all in a school together, learning and playing all kinds of games. It made me so happy to watch them.

I just hope someday that I'll be able to do the same.

ABOUT THE AUTHOR

Aron Beauregard has lived through super dark times. Super dark times that haunt him. Super dark times that aren't over. He has not lived the healthiest lifestyle by any means, and as a result he notices Mr. Bones leering pervishly at him from time to time. He hopes that his work can make an impact on those around him. He hopes, somehow, that it has helped you through your own super dark times.

Made in United States
North Haven, CT
17 June 2024